Happily Ever After
in
Front Royal, Virginia

Missi Magalis

Happily Ever After in Front Royal, Virginia
Copyright © 2017 Missi Magalis
All rights reserved.

Published by Happy Creek Publishing
Front Royal, VA 22630

Library of Congress Control Number: 2017918216
ISBN: 0-9995863-0-0
ISBN-13: 978-0-9995863-0-3

Also by Missi Magalis

Ashmikisle Out of the Ashes

How Do You Do, Mrs. Wiley?

Good Morning, Mrs. Clark

Beautifully Broken

Merry Christmas, Mom and Dad

Ain't No Better Treasure

For Kahle
Brooke, Robin, and Kerry Lane
My everything.
I love you, boys!

And ...

For Christine

God saw a girl in Virginia who needed a girl from Oklahoma.
Thanks for journeying through this life with me.
I am grateful for your love and friendship.

Acknowledgments

If you are reading this page, then the words on it are meant for you. The goodness in me acknowledges and is grateful for the goodness in you. Take care of yourself. How you treat your body is important. What you put in your body is important. What you think is important. Feed your soul only that which is true and wonderful. Recognize your spirit as the powerful entity that it is. Create a positive journey. Remember, your thoughts will not lie to you. Cast off the negative; embrace the positive. The reward is worth it.

Change your mind. Change your world.

☽

This is the first book I've released before sharing a draft with others. Usually, I have people edit for me, and I ask for their feedback, but I chose to complete this novel with minimal assistance. I asked a few questions regarding grammar, but, other than me, no one has read this book before publication. I asked for God's help, and I'm certain He was with me every step of the way. Thanks, God. Also, a huge thank you to Brooke for creating the cover. You really helped me out. And, thank you Kahle, Brooke, Robin, and Kerry Lane for your love and support and for believing in me.

Okay, readers. Here she is ... I am trusting you with yet another of my creations, a child made of pages. I hope you love her as much as I do.

Peace,

Missi

Happily Ever After
in
Front Royal, Virginia

I should've known the end result would be disaster, that Basil Montgomery was simply too good to be true. But, he'd wormed his way far enough into my heart that I'd invited him to dinner to meet my parents. It's not like I need my parents' approval; I want it. But, I didn't get it. Instead, I got a look from my mother that made me want to wither up and get stuck in the crack of the hardwood floor that creaked beneath my foot as I tapped my heel against it, a nervous tic I'd developed at an early age.

One would think that, at my age, I wouldn't care so much. Perhaps I wouldn't have if mother hadn't responded as she did—her lips screwed up like the symbol on a hairpin turn sign, her penciled brows, muddy rainbows, arched so high her hair clouded the tops, her eyes bulging like a cartoon cat being squeezed around the neck.

If mother had said anything but what she'd said, I'd have told her I am my own person, that I love Basil, that I haven't found a single reason to avoid a relationship with him. He keeps his nails trimmed, a pack of gum in his shirt pocket to avoid after dinner onion breath, the radio tuned to my favorite station instead of the awful talk radio show he prefers. He opens doors for me, winks at me from across the table, sends me daisies just because. And, he's cute. So, yes, if mother had simply had a *feeling* something was wrong with Basil, I'd have politely told her, *opinions are exactly like that personal space located below the hips and above the thighs, that very place where the sun don't shine.* Everyone's got one of those just like they've got an opinion. Then, I'd have let Basil Montgomery escort me across the lawn to my cozy little Cape Cod where we'd have enjoyed a cup of hot tea before I told him I was ready to move beyond a kiss.

But, here I sit, at a bar, sipping a now cold Irish coffee, as I replay the evening's events in my mind. Every time I get to the part where Daddy ran after me, I start to tear up. I've always been a daddy's girl. Any other time, I'd have turned back and run right into his arms. Problem is, now I'd feel like I was hugging a stranger.

☽

Evie flings her keys on the bar and orders a sweet tea without ice.

"Sorry I couldn't get here sooner. When you called I was with a client."

By client, my best friend means she was giving a massage. I do not know how she does it—worming people's flesh through her hands for a living—well, for part of a living. I cannot fathom the idea of feeling someone else's skin roll over bone and muscle. *Don't pimples and body hair and body odor and fat and dry skin weird you out?* I've asked on a number of occasions to which she replies that humans are human, that she considers it a privilege that they trust her with their flaws. All I can ever say is, *eww.*

"Must be really bad," Evie says, nodding at my mug. "Let me guess. First drink. Only drink. And you've been here long enough to let it get cold."

I take a swallow. "Yep."

"Not gonna do a thing to take the sting outta whatever's botherin ya."

I look into the mug and swirl the contents as if it might provide a solution.

"So. What's devastated the ever positive outlook of Violet Shine?"

I don't beat around the bush. "I took Basil to meet Mom and Daddy."

"Yeah, so?"

"Things didn't go so well."

"You're forty-three years old, Vi. It doesn't matter what they think. He's a good guy. He's got a great personality, he's self-sufficient, he's gorge—"

"He's..." I interrupt, on the verge of tears. I shake my head and let out a miserable half-laugh before finally saying what I still cannot believe. "He's my brother."

Evie's mouth opens, closes, then opens again—a fish out of water. She motions for the bartender. "Hon," she says pointing to her tea, "I'm gonna need somethin with a little more kick to it than this."

"What's your poison, ma'am?"

"Reckon you could put some lemon in this tea?"

Evie ignores his expression of disbelief, returns her attention to me and prompts, "From the beginning."

☽

Evie knows most of the story. She's the one who got Basil and me together, so I skip over the following:

"There's this guy, Vi. He's a real dreamboat. His eyes are like ... like the color of a mango skin. Beautiful and green and edible."

"Uhm … ew?"

"No. Not ew. Okay, let me see if I can do better. They are like murky river water. Peaceful. Drinkable."

"I don't know anyone who'd drink murky river water."

Evie sighs. "He's drop dead stinkin gorgeous. He's perfect for you. You gotta meet him."

"If he's so great, why are you pawning him off on me?" I ask.

"Because, you are lonely. And I am not."

"Last time I checked we were both single. Not desperate."

"I wasn't implying that either one of us are desperate. It's just that, well … I've been meaning to tell you … I'm sorta seein someone, so I'm off the market. But, you are not. And this guy is just too perfect for you to let him get away."

I disregard the latter to pounce on the news my dearest friend has been keeping from me. "Evelyn Jade Daniels. You are my best friend. How could you keep such a secret?"

"It's a long story." She checks her phone. "And I've got to go to work."

"I wish you'd take a day off every now and then. You are always working."

"I love my job."

I take in her uniform, gray, gray, and more gray, and I compare it to the glow in her cheeks that is there because of the kids she monitors and advises, the ones she sometimes holds in her arms even though she's not supposed to.

"I know you do."

"I'll text you on my break. You've gotta meet him. Even his name is dreamy."

She walks out the door, blowing kisses.

I follow, stand on the porch. She turns to me and smiles wickedly. She knows she's got my curiosity up.

I fold my arms across my chest. "Oh for Pete's sake. What's his name?"

She lowers her voice an octave and says it all breathy. "Basil."

"Basil," I whisper, trying it out on my tongue. It tastes good.

"You're meetin him," she declares, and, I know right then that I will meet him because Evie wants me to. It's not in my nature to disappoint.

"Wait," I say, "I want to hear about your guy."

"Some other time. Gonna be late," she says, ducking inside the car. A second later, the engine revs to life, I hear Jewel crooning from the speakers, and the car and Evie are soon out of sight.

☽

I don't here from Evie until the next morning when her shift is over. She stops by as I'm letting Puck and Harley outside, a German Shepherd and black Siamese cat, respectively, that I've collected from ex's. Evie says the next time I decide to commit to a relationship by taking on the responsibility of a man's pet, that I need to, in her words, "at least name the darn thing after one of *your* hobbies or somethin. That way you don't have to be reminded of the jerk."

I hold the door open for Evie and the dog. The cat is long gone.

"Long night?"

She nods. "Got any coffee?"

"Before bed?"

"You know that doesn't affect me."

"It will any day now," I tell her, but she's already pouring.

"So … Basil," Evie says, not missing a beat.

"Tell me about your night," I say, attempting to avoid Cupid's arrow.

"Just a lot of cryin. Parents suck sometimes."

"What happened?"

"In a nutshell?" Evie sighs. "Sixteen-year-old girl hooked on heroin. In for one too many drug charges and missing too much school. Parents wouldn't even bring her. Said they were too busy. Cops delivered her in cuffs. Beautiful. Smart. And all alone." She sips her coffee savors the flavor for a moment, *Mmms* appreciatively as she swallows, then says, "Now, I wanna talk about Basil."

I relent. Evie needs a distraction, so I will humor her even though I have no desire to meet another man. I haven't had a relationship since Drew the biker. He and I adopted Harley, and he's almost four. I attract the unfaithful, the liars, the abusers. Drew was all three. Did me in. Alone is peaceful. It is quiet. It doesn't screw you over. But, I will hear out my friend because I love her. But not before throwing her a curve ball.

"What about *your* boyfriend? I wanna hear about him."

"Later. Basil is time sensitive."

"What do you mean?"

"I told him I'd bring you to meet him this afternoon after my shut-eye."

"What?" I shriek like a teenager.

"Oh, shut-up. Listen, I wouldn't lead you astray. This one's a keeper. I feel it in my bones." Evie jiggles her shoulders to insinuate her bones are feeling something.

I roll my eyes and top off my own coffee and hers. "Spill it," I say, and pull a stool next to hers.

"I met him at the big yard sale place down there by the gas station that has a Duncan Donuts. He was sellin his art work, and boy let me tell you, he does beautiful work."

Evie has lived here oh, about twenty years, long enough to pick up the local accent and know the place like the back of her hand. But, she's never been one to commit names and places to memory. Me, I've lived in Front Royal my whole life. I know every nook and cranny of this storybook town.

"Are you talkin about the flea market on Commerce Avenue, right next to the Exxon station?" I ask.

"Yeah!" she exclaims overly energetic for someone who's worked all night. "Margaret from work, the one with the two gold front teeth that you met at the Christmas party last year ... you know who I'm talking about, right?"

"Emmhmm."

"She wanted to check out the produce there. I was all prepared for a boring time but then Basil introduced himself and all I could think about was how I had to introduce the two of you. I told him about you and how you fiddle around with paintin and drawin sometimes."

"You didn't!"

"Sure did. He's only here for a few months. Travels from place to place paintin and sellin his work. He says he makes enough to get by and that if he never makes it

17

in the art world, he's perfectly content the way things are. Says it's excitin seeing all the new places and faces but that he sometimes wants to settle down."

I shake my head. "Sounds like a drifter. I don't need that kind of headache, Eaves."

"You might be the one to settle him down. Or, he may be a stepping stone, you know, what you need to get back in the dating game. Come on," she pleads. "I've got a good feelin about this."

To Evie's credit, she's never tried to hook me up with anyone, and her *feelings* are usually spot on. I chew my bottom lip, thinking.

She drains her coffee and smiles. "I'll just sleep here. Get me up at two so I can shower before we go. I told him we'd meet him at four."

I stand up, brace myself on the tortoise tile countertop. "Wait? I didn't say I'd go."

"I know you will though. And, look at ya. You're chewin your lip. That means yes." She stifles a yawn. "So tired." And heads for my room. "Two," she reminds me and closes my bedroom door.

☽

Evie showers and dons a pair of my jeans along with a thermal and a faded Old Navy sweatshirt I've had forever.

"Ready?" she asks as she squeezes her foot into a pair of my boots and mutters about the inconvenience of my feet being a half size smaller than hers.

"Maybe you should leave some of *your* stuff here," I suggest, "and bring my stuff back." This isn't the first time she's slept here after work.

Evie picks up a muffin that's recently come out of the oven and takes a bite as she grabs her keys. "Heaven just hit my taste buds, Violet. Who are these for?"

"One's for you, obviously," I say, pulling on my coat and following her out. "The others are a donation for a Girl Scout bake sale."

"But you're not a Girl Scout."

"Fran's kid is. She asked if I'd make some."

"Because she's too lazy to make them herself."

"She said it's because she likes my muffins."

Evie harrumphs. I change the subject. "Where are we meeting this guy?"

"Crazy Wyllie's."

I should've known. Evie loves ice cream. Doesn't matter that the beginning of March is being a freezing witch. Any occasion is an excuse for ice cream in Evie's world. It's a wonder she stays so fit.

"So, tell me about your guy," I try again as we make the two minute trip to C&C's.

"Not now, Vi."

"Why not?"

"Because now is your time to meet someone."

"Why are you being so pushy about this?"

"Like I said, I've got a feelin. If he's *the* one, you need to get goin with him before he up and leaves. Who knows, maybe he'll ask you to travel with him."

"Right," I mutter as she pulls up across the street from shop.

Evie and I wait for Basil for the better part of an hour and have just decided to place a to-go order when he finally shows up. All I'm thinking is how punctual I am and how irritated I'd be if this guy asked me out on a date and then showed up late. But, he has a great excuse.

"Work," he says, hugging Evie before taking my hand and kissing it. "I had to finish a landscape. Had just the right color mixed up and the light was perfect, and, well, to be honest, I was in the zone." He's talking to Evie while staring straight into my soul. He smiles at me and says, "You must be Violet."

His eyes sparkle like magic shamrocks. I filed away the comparison for later when Evie and I will go over every detail.

"Basil Montgomery," he says. "I am so sorry to have wasted your time. I always say when someone's late it means they believe their time to be more important than yours. Believe me ladies that is not true in this case. I should've called. But then I thought that'd just take more time. All around poor first impression, I'm sure." He takes a breath. "Let me buy your ice cream."

Evie tells him the rule, "No vanilla, chocolate, or strawberry unless you try three original flavors first."

"Who wants boring vanilla when I can get *I don't know* and *I don't care?*" he says, reading the flavor titles posted on the freezer case. "I'll have a scoop of each of those."

I order my favorite, brownie batter and kettle corn, and Evie gets her usual, two scoops of lemon cookie in a cone.

"So … Evie tells me you are looking for some companionship."

It's a good thing I have ice cream to cool me off because my face flushes hot. "She did, did she?"

"Yeah, she says you're a lonely middle-aged woman who wallows in self-pity all day, reading your horoscope and searching for men on the Internet."

"Evelyn Jade!" I exclaim and start to get up. I'm not sure what I am going to do, leave maybe, but then

Basil cracks a wide grin that makes his eyes crinkle devilishly.

"I'm teasing," he says. "Sit. Please." He stands until I am seated again.

"Actually, in the few minutes we spoke, your friend told me that you are quite the artist yourself and that I should see some of your work."

"I just play around. I have no clue what I'm doing, really. Sometimes I finger paint. It's just a hobby."

Basil smiles. "That's what they all say."

"Who?"

"All the best artists."

"I'm hardly a painter. I do all kinds of other stuff."

"Like what?"

I feel put on the spot, and suddenly, I can't think of a single thing to tell him. *Who am I?* I ask myself as I take a bite of ice cream. *How do I describe myself? I have no idea.*

I can't tell him I'm the girl who won the lottery on her nineteenth birthday. Enough to take care of myself and my parents and anyone else I want to take care of for the rest of my life and beyond. Then he'd just want my money. I can't tell him that I volunteer at the library and the hospital and at the church and that I teach crochet to some ladies at a senior center. I can't tell him that I begin my day with a walk or a hike and that, unless I have an obligation, I go next door to help my parents with whatever they need, and then putz around at home cleaning or creating something whether it be food or art. Or that sometimes I go out to lunch or to the movies by myself. I can't tell him I'm usually in bed by eight in the winter, hunkered down with a good book and a cup of chamomile tea. That in the summer I garden until the sun goes down. I can't tell him that I do have worries. I worry about my parents getting old. And I worry about Evie who works her tail cheeks off to make ends meet while also sending money to her two kids whenever they call begging. I can't tell him all these things because he will think me superficial and silly. Me, the middle-aged woman who has never had a real job.

"Violet," Evie calls, shaking me from my thoughts.

"Wh-what?"

"Where'd you go?" Basil asks.

"Just thinking."

I look down into the puddle my ice cream has become and decide right then that I am not going to hide a thing. Not even my poor manners. I pick up the bowl of ice cream and begin to drink it. When I'm finished, I wipe my face with my bare hand and then slide it along my jeans.

"Here's the truth, Basil. Evie here wants us to go out. She has a *feeling* we are meant for each other. You are a wandering artist who does not want to settle down with a girl like me. I've been hurt by too many men. I'm cautious and somewhat bitter. Simply put, I'm an average gal with a boat load of money. When men find out, they want to date me. When they find out I'm not willing to be their sugar momma, they split.

"I spend my days doing whatever strikes me as the thing to do. I'm boring, really." I shrug and stand to leave. "Evie was wrong to have set this up." I look at my best friend. "I'm gonna walk back, Eaves."

Before either of them can protest, I've dropped my bowl in the trash and am halfway up Main Street.

☽

An hour later, there's a knock on my door. Thinking Evie has come to give me a *what fer* for being so rude to her friend, I don't think twice about answering in my too-short flannel nightgown.

"Before you blame Evie, I want you to know I googled your address," Basil says through the storm door I refuse to open.

What if he's a serial killer? What if he's come to rob me? I am so stupid for brazenly announcing that I have money, I berate myself. But, when his teeth begin chattering, I decide I've taken enough kickboxing classes in my lifetime. I'd be able to knock the breath out of him and run away if he tries to murder me. And, my money is secure in a bank across town, except the stash I divvy up in the bellies of spices I haven't used in years. I swallow my imagination and release the latch.

"Hot chocolate?" I query, letting him in.

"Sounds great."

"Why are you here?"

"Evie's feeling," he says. I give him my best *that's ridiculous* look. "And ... you're interesting."

"Interesting." I say the word. It tastes foreign when mixed with equal parts me. "That's hardly how I'd describe myself."

"Well, then. Let me describe you."

"You don't know me."

"I'm an artist. I read people well."

I place a mug in front of him. It is painted in hundreds of tiny rainbows. I made it myself, but I won't tell him this. He'll surely see the flaws.

23

"I'm not a book," I say.

"No. You are an epic poem. Beautiful. Complicated. Worth reading time and again."

We sit in silence, sipping, until finally, Basil reaches for my hand. I jerk mine away.

"You've been hurt. I get that." He unbuttons the coat I did not offer to take. "It's hotter than satan's toenails in here," he says.

I laugh.

"Aw. A smile. It lights up your face."

I angle my head at him, feeling very girlishly mushy at the compliment. "What do you want?"

"Nothing. Well, that's not true. I want your friendship. Evie said you know this town better than anyone. I'm here for a little while. I'd like to be your friend. And I'd like to learn about this town I'm trying to paint."

"That's it?"

He nods. "I don't want your money. And I will never think you any less of a person because you don't have to work. After you left, Evie told me how busy you are, all that you do in a day. More than many who have full-time jobs. I'm not going to think less of you because you have financial stability."

"Stability I didn't have to work for," I add. "It's that specific blessing that makes me feel guilty sometimes."

"It'd be different if you were a liar or a cheat or a squandering fool. But, according to Evie, you are none of those. Feeling guilty about winning the lottery … well, that's absurd."

"Gee thanks," I say, not able to discern if what he said is meant as a compliment or a criticism. Perhaps, a little of both.

"I don't mean *you* are absurd. I simply mean you are a good person who deserves the best. Something good happened to you. And it's made your life a little easier. So what? You shouldn't feel guilty about anything."

Just as I am about to ask how, in the little time he's known me, he has come to the conclusion that I am a good person, Puck wanders out to see why I've not made my way back to the bedroom. He takes a sniff of Basil's pants and disappears back the hall, his brief interruption enough to end this uncomfortable line of conversation.

"Fierce attack dog, that one."

We laugh.

"Call me?" he asks, retrieving a pen from a vase with a willow tree painted on the front. I'd worked on that thing for months trying to get the leaves just perfect. Basil writes his number under my current grocery list I've left on the counter and returns the pen to its spot. "Only if you can't meet me at the gazebo tomorrow morning to show me around. Otherwise, I'll see you there. Nine o'clock sharp."

He buttons his coat, rinses his mug in the sink. "Your work is amazing," he says holding up the mug, searching out the vase, running his finger along a bookshelf I built myself. I burned the titles of all my favorite books all over the frame.

"When do I get to see your work?" I ask feeling vulnerable as he studies my very amateur attempts at art.

"Someday." And with that, he turns and leaves.

☽

I never wanted a big house, but my parents did. So, the minute my winnings were deposited in my bank account, I snatched up an empty lot with a twenty-year-old Cape

Cod situated on the property in such a way that I had a humdinger built for Mom and Daddy on the corner, and I took up residence right next door. I explain all this to Basil as I walk with him in town. I also admit my need for the ordinary and simple as I point out the old library on Chester Street. "Fancy stuff makes me feel lonely," I admit.

"Let me guess. Before the lottery, you didn't have much, but you were happy."

I smile and nod. "Incredible," I say of Basil's accuracy.

We stop in front of Dad's pawnshop, *Sea More Bright Side Pawn* (*exchange your half-full glass for a cup overflowing*) at the corner of Chester and Main. I point out Daddy's business.

"Want to go in?" he asks.

"You know what I really want? A cup of coffee. We've been walking for more than an hour. I'm chilly."

"Good idea."

We move along, making our way up Main Street to Daily Grind. We've just placed our order and seated ourselves in overstuffed chairs while the barista whips up our drinks, when Evie rushes in. She sees us and hurries over to compliment me on my Humpty-Dumptiness, as she puts it.

"You sealed your cracks and climbed back up on the wall all by yourself, I see." She's talking about my rude departure yesterday and how it appears I've gotten over myself.

"Basil came by last night," I say. "Everything's okay now. I may have been a little—"

"Uptight?" she calls over her shoulder as she walks to the counter to order. She returns with her own coffee and ours.

"He wants the three of us to go out to dinner Friday," I tell her. "You good with that?"

Evie looks up, tilts her head slightly, right then left, counting the days in her head. "Yep. I'm off this weekend." She checks her watch. "Right now, though, I'm running late. Gotta go."

"You just got here."

"Yeah, and I didn't know you were gonna be here. It's not like we were meetin for lunch," she snaps.

"Wow," I say, stunned at the abrupt change in Evie's tone. That came outta nowhere. What's wrong?"

"Nothin."

"*Something's* wrong. You just bit my head off."

She sighs. "Joe put his fist through the windshield of his car last night."

"No he did not," I say, sitting up a little straighter.

Evie nods. "Got in a fight with his girlfriend."

I want to say that she should not foot this bill, but I don't. I want to offer to help so that she doesn't have to rob Peter to pay Paul. But I don't. I've tried meddling on too many occasions, and she always shuts me down. She refuses to accept money from me, says it's not okay. When I try to help, she usually gets mad. So, I say nothing. Well, almost nothing. "Joe needs to grow up."

"You're not kidding," she states matter-of-factly before kissing my cheek and hugging Basil. "Sorry for bein a brat. See ya."

She's not out the door two seconds and Basil and I are both talking at once.

"Who's Joe?" he asks at the same time I say, "Scum bag."

I sigh. "Joe is Evie's son. He lives in Florida. I hate to say it, but he's a turd. Evie is always bailing him outta something."

"How old?"

"Twenty-two? I think."

"I didn't know Evie is married."

"She's not. Neither of us have ever tied the knot."

Before Basil can ask further questions, I hold a hand up and say, "It's not my story to share. Evie'll tell you all about it, I'm sure. She's an open book."

"And you're not."

I shrug. "I promised to vacuum the church this afternoon, so I better get goin."

He takes me back to my house to pick up my car. "Mind if I come by after work tomorrow?"

"For?"

"Some company? I'll bring some canvas and show you a few things. If you want."

I had mentioned wanting to hone my painting skills.

"Sure," I agree. "That'd be fun."

☽

For the next few weeks, Basil, Evie, and I form a trio. When Evie is working, Basil and I are the dynamic art duo. After he's completed his serious art hours for the day—his work, he teaches me about lines and shading, and I teach him to crochet. He's determined to finish two scarfs before he takes off for another town. "Christmas for Mom and Dad," he says.

We've been to the movies to see *Fist Fight* and *Beauty and the Beast*, eaten our share of People's Fries at Pavemint, and hiked miles and miles on Skyline Drive. We've cooked together, painted, drawn, cooked and painted some more. Some evenings, we work on refinishing an old dresser I had when I was a kid.

This afternoon, we are finger painting.

"When do I get to meet your parents?" Basil asks.

Before he arrived, he'd been painting outdoors. He smells of earth and chocolate.

I ignore him. "I need to get some green." I rummage through the art closet searching even though I know exactly where the green is.

Basil's been here enough to know the closet well. He reaches above my head and pulls a jar of green finger-paint from the second shelf.

"You're avoiding the question," he says as he unscrews the lid and scoops green onto the palette.

I roll my neck and stretch my back. "If I take you to meet Mom and Dad, they'll … it's complicated."

Basil separates the paper, places one in front of me, reaches and dips two fingers in black and draws a half-circle.

"They'll think we're together," he states.

I nod. "And I don't want to explain." I draw some green circles on my page, then squiggly brown trunks that remind me of Dr. Seuss. "I feel like a child," I say.

"That's a good thing."

I relax. "Basil … I think you're right. You should meet my parents."

"No, it's fine."

"You're my friend."

Basil changes the subject. "What's your favorite color?"

"What's yours?" I challenge. I find a favorite color to be one of the most intimate pieces of information about a person. I'm not sure if I'm ready to share this with him.

Over the past weeks, I've learned that I miss Basil when he's at work and that I look forward to hearing "Hello. Anyone home?" when he comes over.

Once, he left behind one of his sweatshirts, and, silly-girl-at-heart that I am, I slept in it. Truth is, I don't want to introduce Basil to my parents because I don't want to tell them that he's only a friend.

"Midnight blue," Basil answers.

"Huh?"

"My favorite color."

"Oh. Right."

"Where were you just now?"

I laugh. "Thinkin about this painting," I say. I look down to find I've drawn red swirls around the trees, a sky at the tree roots, and the grass in the sky.

"Why midnight blue?" I ask.

"Because you can create anything out of it. Stars, moon, clouds, a table with ripe fruit in a bowl, two people holding hands. Anything. Midnight blue makes an excellent foundation."

I think of my painting that has no background. I just started painting objects. I look at his, black fading to deep blue then lighter and lighter with a deep orange sun slightly off center.

"Mine's yellow," I offer up, my vulnerability wedged in my throat, or is that my heart?

"Oh? Why yellow?"

Before I consider the why of it, I blurt out, "It's the promise of all things good. Joy and love and hope and peace."

"You're beautiful, you know that?" Basil asks.

I blush and look down at my painting. It needs a sky. I reach for midnight blue; Basil has his fingers in the yellow. It seems we are trying on the other's ideas, like wearing shoes that feel funny but are somehow warm and comfortable all at the same time.

Basil comes around the table. In the next instant my face is in his hands and he's kissing me. I let my eyes close and really feel the moment. I grab hold of his shirt front but feel unsteady, nonetheless.

The doorbell, followed by a knock, ends the moment. It's Fran.

"Well, if you aren't a mess," she observes as I open the door for her to come in.

I reach up and touch the half-dry yellow on my cheek. The mark of Basil. He joins me, a deep blue stain added to the other colors on his smock. He's wiping his hands with a rag.

"Well, who's this?" Fran inquires.

I introduce them.

"What's up, Fran?" I ask.

"The men's group at my church would just love it if you'd make some of your apple cinnamon muffins for their breakfast. Fred bought some at the Girl Scout bake sale. He said they'd pay you for them."

"Nonsense. When do you need them?"

"Tomorrow," she says, an apology in her tone. "I meant to call sooner, but with the twins and Tommy and, well … it's been busy."

Fran is always busy.

"Want to pick em up later on this evening? Say around eight?" I am hoping for a little more alone time with Basil before getting to work on the muffins.

"Would you mind dropping them by the church early tomorrow morning? Fred said he'll be there at 6:30."

I smile. "Sure, Fran."

"Great. Mind if I hide here while you make em? That way Tommy'll have to take the girls to soccer." I try not to look disappointed.

Basil, clearly my champion, says, "If you're staying, you can take them with you."

"Fred wants them in the morning, and I cannot get out there first thing. Not with the twins. I suppose I could take them by tonight, but his house is in the opposite direction of mine. Too much trouble," she says.

"Let me just go clean up the paint, and I'll be right out."

"I'll just make myself at home," Fran says, pulling a glass off the shelf.

Basil follows me to my art room.

"Wow."

"What?" I ask.

"She always like that?"

"Like what?"

"Pushy."

"She's busy. I'm not."

Basil turns me to face him.

"Just because you aren't married with twins doesn't make your life any less important."

I place my hands on his chest. "Thank you."

"For what?"

"For sayin that."

"Need some help with those muffins?"

"Nah. But I suppose I should get started."

I look at our half-finished work. His, a universe that consists of a lonely sun surrounded by darkness, and mine, trees and bright color minus the stability of a background. *What these pictures could be if they were blended*, I think to myself.

We clean up in silence, leave our paintings to finish drying. Basil stops me before I can head to the kitchen.

"I like you, Violet. A lot. More than a friend, a lot."

32

My heart turns cartwheels in my chest.

"You can tell your parents we are more than friends."

How is it this man knows my most personal thoughts without my ever having to voice them?

I touch my nose to his. "I think you should meet them."

He kisses me again.

"Vi? You have any coffee? I think I'd like some. Or maybe a hot tea. Water ain't cuttin it."

"Pushy," Basil whispers, and gives my hand a squeeze.

My insides feel like they are blooming wild flowers. I am so happy.

"I'll text you later with some dates for dinner with my parents."

Basil winks at me and calls good-bye to Fran as he pushes his feet into his shoes and leaves.

☽

That's the part Evie knows about; here's the part that's news to her:

Two days after the kiss, Basil meets me at my house before heading to Mom and Dad's for dinner.

"They are so excited to meet you," I tell him as he checks his hair and beard in the mirror.

"Think I should shave it off?" he asks of his beard, to which I reply with an emphatic no.

"Now, I have to warn you, Mom's a little put out because I've let her assume the bus driving friend of mine is a woman. I mean, I didn't come out and say that, but I didn't not say it either."

"Does your mother not peep through her blinds? Surely, she's seen me coming and going by now."

"I'd have thought so, too, but, miraculously she hasn't. And if Daddy did, he didn't say. He's good about my privacy." I take a deep cleansing breath to settle the butterflies that are fluttering with more gusto the closer it gets to dinner, then add, "We are having spaghetti and meatballs. Hope that's okay."

Basil looks down at the white shirt he's wearing with a pair of khaki shorts. "I'm a spaghetti slob," he says and shrugs. "But, I'm sure it'll be fine."

I look at the clock. Ten of five. "Time to head over."

We leave out the side entrance off of the kitchen, circle around the front, cross my lawn and theirs. It is a beautiful spring evening. Hard to believe that only three weeks ago it was freezing.

At the door, Basil touches my elbow. I turn into a kiss that makes my insides catch fire.

"That's to say thank you."

"For what?"

"For allowing me into your life when mine is so … uncertain."

He's talking about leaving, I know, but I refuse to think about that. Not now. I take his hand and give it a squeeze, then I open the door and holler as we step into the foyer. "Hello. It's me."

"Hello, Moonbeam," Daddy calls from somewhere in the bowels of the house, probably the kitchen. The joy in his voice is full and round, like the biggest bubble I ever blew. Unfortunately, that big bubble of joy pops as soon as he enters the foyer and reaches for Basil's hand. I swear you'd have thought Basil had horns or boils on his face or a second nose. That's how quickly Daddy's mouth turns into the most exaggerated *n* I've ever seen.

34

"D-daddy? Uhm, this is Basil. Basil, my daddy, Seamore Shine, but everyone calls him Sea."

"Nice to meet you, Mr. Shine."

Daddy doesn't say a word. It's like his spit turned to glue and sealed his lips shut. "Daddy? Are you okay?"

For the first time ever, Daddy is all but speechless. The only word he is able to mutter is my mother's name.

You ever recall being really scared? You want to scream and run, but your words come out in a whisper, and your shoes are cement blocks? It happened to me once in the fourth grade when this great big tall girl threatened me on the playground. I couldn't move. Thankfully, the teacher blew the whistle for recess to end. The girl ran off. It took a minute for my legs to work properly. I was late getting back to class. My knees were shaking so badly. That's how Daddy's acting right now—like he's stuck.

Annoyed and uncertain as to how to respond to such rude and unpredictable behavior, I take Basil's hand and lead him to the kitchen, leaving Daddy to figure a way out of his cement shoes. "Mom, we're here," I say, even though I'm sure she heard me holler hello.

Her back is to us. She is stirring a delicious smelling meat sauce and humming a tune, I think that "Casey Jones" song by the Grateful Dead. She is totally absorbed in her own world and clearly hasn't heard us come in as I'd thought. She lifts the pot to transfer it to the island, and, as she turns, it is as if time slips into slow motion.

"Mom, this is Basil," I say and follow with, "Basil, this is my mom, Hardy."

Basil steps forward to hug my mother. It is then that I notice Daddy has made his way back to the kitchen, rounding the island, rushing to get to Mom. The smile she has on her face turns to an *O* of shock. And then, like that mom on Matilda who throws the cereal everywhere when her husband comes in with his hair dyed, well, that's what Mom does with the hot spaghetti sauce. If Daddy had made it two steps closer, he'd have been on his way to the hospital for second degree burns. Instead, he slips in the mess and falls backward, hurting his pride more than anything else.

Basil extends his hand, helps Daddy up.

"Seems I'm causing quite a stir," he says. "Either that, or there's some Virginia greeting custom I don't know about." He chuckles at his own joke, but Mom and Daddy do not join in.

I am furious. "What is the matter with you two?" I demand.

"Violet." Mom stops and starts, looks at Daddy, "Sea?" She says his name in a question, a cry for help.

My stomach flips over, but I don't know why. It dawns on me that something is very wrong.

Daddy finds his voice. "Are you two an," he raises a fist and coughs into it, "an item?"

My face flames red. Basil and I haven't discussed the terms of our relationship. I don't really know what to say.

Basil speaks up. "I like your daughter very much. We've got a lot in common. I don't know where this," he points to me and then himself, "is going, but I do have feelings for Violet."

Silence. The only sound is the splat of sauce dripping from the island to the floor.

Now I'm really mad. "Look, I don't know what's gotten into you two, but you're both being very rude. I am so sorry, Basil. Let's go," I say and turn to leave.

But Daddy stops me.

"We have to tell her—them," he corrects. "We have no other choice."

I turn back, place a fist on my hip, something Daddy does when he's upset. "Tell us what?"

"Moonbeam," Mom says, "You better sit down."

☽

"So we sat down around the island," I recount to Evie, drink the last of my cold coffee, and ask the bartender for an ice water. "I should've known it was really bad news. Mom wasn't even trying to clean up the sauce.

"Daddy vanished, I thought to change shirts since he got some of the sauce splatter. I sat there mortified, not able to make eye contact with Basil. I was a millisecond away from getting up and walking out, when Daddy came back still wearing his stained shirt. He hadn't gone to change after all. He'd gone to get a box.

"Mom took it from him. I tell you, Evie, the way they looked at each other, you'd have thought that box had a bomb in it." I shake my head and grunt. "It actually did."

"What was in it?"

"Pictures. Tons of pictures."

"Of?"

"Basil and Trip. Pictures of them from the time they were newborns."

Evie's face is so scrunched in sympathy, I can't see her eyes.

"I have two twin brothers. Not one, but two. Can you believe that?"

All Evie can do is shake her head. "Did someone kidnap the boys? But then why would your parents have pictures?"

I put Evie out of her misery. "We aren't Daddy's kids. Not biologically, anyway." Vocalizing this fact makes me feel queasy.

"What?" Evie's voice goes so high it puts me to mind of a strong wind lifting a kite.

"Mom had a fling with some stray before she met Daddy—a one night stand. She had us and knew she couldn't provide a good life for triplets. She was planning to give us all up for adoption, but when she was about to hand me over to the nurse, I latched onto her finger and started screamin. The only way I'd calm down is if she put my ear on her heart.

"She kept me, got a second job at a country store. She'd work all day doin accounting, pick me up at four from the babysitter, then work half the night at the store.

"When I was six months old, Daddy stopped at the store for some gas. He'd been in town fishing with an old friend. When he went in to pay, Mom was singin to me. He said he fell in love with both of us right then and there. Shut down his business in South Carolina and opened another pawnshop here where he could be with Mom."

I spin my glass in a circle, take a long drink of water, then finish with, "I heard all this over voice mail."

"What do you mean?"

"I mean as soon as Mom showed me the pictures, I ran out of the house. I stayed in a hotel last night so they wouldn't pester me. They left one message right after the other. Mom, Daddy, Basil. Between the three of them, I got the story. Basil must've stayed after I left. I hate that I abandoned him, but I couldn't look at him." My eyes fill with tears of loss and embarrassment. "I was really starting to like him, really like him."

Evie covers my hand with hers. "You can still like him, Vi. Love him, even. As a brother."

I look at her, my eyes brimming, and say again, "I kissed my brother."

She hands me a napkin. I wipe away the tears.

"Yeah," Evie says. "That's cringe worthy."

Two fat tears slide down my cheeks as I let out a laugh.

☾

I stay with Evie for two days. I text Daddy, let him know I'm safe, check on the animals that I know he's been taking care of even though I didn't ask. He tells me they're fine, asks if we can talk. I do not respond.

I cannot bring myself to communicate, in any way, with to Mom or Basil. Don't know why. The awkwardness of the situation, maybe? Anger at having the wool pulled over my eyes all these years? I don't know. Part of me thinks Mom should've told me; the other part wishes I still didn't know.

And Basil, well ... I'm still thinking of that kiss and wishing it hadn't affected me the way it had. Of course, now, the thought of his lips on mine makes my stomach churn like I've eaten bad fish. Shouldn't I have sensed somehow that we weren't meant for one another? I mean, my goodness. He. Is. My. Brother. And we kissed. Well, the fire it caused in me has been doused and drowned with more than a bucketful of shame and embarrassment, that's for sure. Still, his latest message has me thinking of going home.

Violet, it's me, your almost boyfriend turned brother here. I want to see you. We need to talk. This is a strange situation, indeed. What do you say we get the awkward meeting out of the way? I'll be swinging by your parents' after work. Why don't you meet me there? Don't worry. You won't be the only one who has trouble making eye contact.

I hadn't really considered that Basil would be feeling the same as me. Embarrassed. Confused over the feelings we'd started to develop that are most certainly gone now. The transition that'd have to be made. But … do we even want a relationship as brother and sister? And what about the other brother? Trip. I think of the pictures I saw. Try to envision the similarities, but I can't make it happen. Not in my head.

When Evie gets home from giving three massages, she offers a freebie to me. I take her up on it. I tell her about Basil's message.

"You need to go home," she says as she digs her elbow into my back and slides it around the comma of my shoulder blade.

I groan.

"It's been nice havin the company, but you've worn just about all of your clothes that I've borrowed."

I start to roll over, but Evie digs her elbow into the other side.

I groan again.

Through with my back, Evie makes her way to the little dresser where she keeps her lotions, returning with a palmful she begins working into my legs. "When you wouldn't answer the phone, your mom called. I assured her you were fine and that you'd be home today."

I sit up, pull the sheet over my chest. "Why did you tell her that?"

"Because Basil said he was meeting with you this afternoon."

"You've talked to Basil?"

"Why wouldn't I talk to Basil?"

In all of my self-pity, I'd completely dismissed any thought of communication between Evie and my family. Basil included.

"What makes you think I'm going to meet him?"

"Because I'm kicking you out."

My shoulders suddenly feel very heavy. I hunch forward, stare at the sheet. Whiter than my own fair complexion.

"I don't have to go home," I mutter.

"Yes you do. You know you have to face this. You are not one to run from your problems." She pushes me back, tells me to turn over. "You can go after your massage."

Evie is right. I've never run from anything. Though, to be fair, there's not been anything in my life to run from. I mean, I'm a go getter. I guess. I've been to town meetings to speak up about bricking Main Street. I speak out against animal cruelty on Facebook.

Also, I'm not afraid to intervene in altercations. Like the time this guy was shaking the bejesus out of his girlfriend in a restaurant parking lot. I asked him to please stop. When he said, "Mind your f-ing business," something in me got really heated. I balled up my fist and coldcocked the guy. Knocked him on his derriere. I thought the girl would be pleased, but before I could turn around to see if she needed a ride, she was on my back yanking my hair. I could not for the life of me understand why she was all up in arms with yours truly. The police showed up just as I flipped her over my head. When I explained the situation and told him about the thanks I did not get, the officer nodded. "Happens more than you can imagine."

I never knew that women take up for their attacker like that. The experience prompted me to volunteer at the shelter for battered and abused women and children. I can't begin to guess the number of times I've said, "It is not okay to pull hair." That crap really hurt. I also tell them not to take up for their piece of crap abuser, but, ultimately, they have to figure that out themselves. Sometimes they come around; sometimes not. So, no, I suppose I don't run from a challenge.

But, all things considered, I've lived a charmed life. This is the first truly horrific storm that's flooded my soul, left me waterlogged and pruned. But, the more I think about it, as I am swallowed by the delicious pain of Evie's strong hands, the more I wonder why this has to be a bad situation.

Of course, the town tongues will wag for ages. And then, it dawns on me: The only thing I've ever really worried about is what other people think. Suddenly, I am wondering why that should even be a thing.

"Feelin better?" Evie asks as she finishes massaging the last of my toes.

I flip over, sit up, and smile. "Yeah. I am."

I tuck a corner of the sheet and head to the bathroom. "Thanks for kickin me out," I say over my shoulder as I close the door on my previous life and make room in my heart for another.

☽

I piddle around at Evie's for a bit. Who am I kidding? I piddle around a lot. I make her a pot of tortilla soup for dinner, then I stay for dinner, then I clean up after dinner. It is dark outside and I am tired and ready for my own bed by the time I slip through the side door of my own home and, without turning on any lights, feel my way past the peninsula and living room wall, and take a left down the hall to my room. Puck is on the edge of my bed. He does not greet me, nor does he move when I peel back the covers and sigh into my pillow.

I sleep until I am aware of a presence. I open one eye and watch as Daddy tries to gently coax Puck off the bed gently so as not to wake me.

"Mornin," I mumble.

Daddy jumps as if I've shot at him and the bullet grazed his ear.

"Lord have mercy, Vi," he says, holding his heart. "You nearly gave me a heart attack."

"Didn't you see me?" I ask, stretching slightly before emerging from my comfortable cocoon.

"I thought you were asleep."

I press my palms into the mattress, zero in on a hangnail, let the silence waltz between us. Without looking up, I finally manage, "I'm sorry I ran off like that."

He clears his throat. "Moonbeam," he says softly. "You will always be my daughter. No matter what. Nothing will ever change that."

I fly into his arms and cry all over his polo shirt, leaving behind mascara smudges I know Mom will stain stick as soon as she sees the mess.

☽

I walk across the lawn at quarter till five, retracing my steps from a few nights ago. Basil's bus is parked in the driveway. Out of nowhere, a wave of jealousy snakes its way from my heart down into the pit of my stomach. I find myself questioning this reaction. Why should I be jealous? Over having to share Mom? Or Basil? Or, perhaps it isn't jealousy at all. Maybe, it is regret that relationships have been forever altered. Yes, that's it. Regret along with the mortification I cannot seem to shake. Basil and I spent weeks falling for each other. And, holy cow ... that kiss. How awful.

I send up a prayer for strength and open the door. They are in the kitchen talking quietly enough that only every third word or so is clear. I pause at the kitchen doorway. Mom has an arm draped over Basil's shoulders, sheer joy flushing her cheeks. It is clear she's dreamed of this reunion, probably not in the way it occurred, but she is happy, nonetheless.

Basil and Daddy are pulling pictures from the old cream colored box I recognize from a few nights ago— Mom's secret picture stash of Basil and my other brother.

My breath catches when Basil lifts his cheek from his hand and turns toward me. He has shaved. Now, as we stare at one another, I wonder how we could have missed the resemblance.

"Vi," he says softly.

Mom and Daddy look up. Just like earlier with Daddy, I am in my mother's arms in less than a heartbeat. Her soft gray curls tickle my nose, and I sneeze.

"I'm so sorry, Moonbeam," and I know she is talking about more than her unruly hair getting in the way.

I breathe in the scent of her and relax a bit. "Two brothers, huh?" I say on the exhale.

Mom places a hand in the center of my back, rubs in a clockwise pattern, something she's done to comfort me for as long as I can remember. The familiarity calms me.

"Yep," she says, releasing me and making her way back to the island, motioning for me to follow.

"I thought about coming to talk to you today, but I didn't know what to say," she admits. The room is silent but for the ceiling fan clicking as it turns. Mom stares at the pictures covering the counter, and adds, "Still don't."

"I'm not mad. Not anymore," I say.

Mom looks at me, relief and gratitude erasing the worry lines that were present around her mouth and eyes seconds ago.

I stop a few paces from Basil. He reaches for my hand. I place mine in his.

"Sis," he says, trying out the word much like one tastes a new flavor of hard candy. His grin tells me he enjoys it.

I lean my shoulder against his, then turn to face him, scouring his features. "Gosh, we look alike."

☽

Mom and Daddy take turns telling the story I'd pieced together from the voice mails, showing me pictures of Basil Montgomery and Trip Wilson.

"You don't have as many pictures of Trip," I notice, searching the blue eyes of a toddler, the right one squinting just like Mom's does when she smiles, for any resemblance to Basil or me.

"His parents divorced. He moved to Nosilla, New York with his father. It's a sliver of a place, not very big at all, situated between Brooklyn and Manhattan. I went there."

"You did?"

"Remember that trip I took to become an Avon lady?"

I nod.

"Remember how I never became one?"

I nod again.

"Well, that's because I wasn't at Avon training. I wanted to see with my own two eyes where my son was bein raised. I was back and forth between Brooklyn and Manhattan for hours lookin for that little place. It's named after a famous playwright, you know. I met the sweet gal in a restaurant when I visited. Stunning. And so sweet. We shared a table. She told me how she used to bike from Brooklyn to Manhattan when she was a student. And wouldn't you know, she's so down-to-earth, she didn't even tell me who she is. I found that out later when I stopped at a restaurant named in her honor. Her picture hangs behind the bar."

Mom stops, realizing she's digressed.

"Anyway, I simply drove by to see if I could get a peek of the place where Trip lived. I had no intention of seeking him out. Just a mother's yearning to see her son was safe. I waited a while, but I never saw him."

She looks to Basil. "I flew to your place next. Only the one time. Idaho is beautiful. And, your parents' farm ... well, it's breathtaking."

A smile plays across Basil's features. I wonder if he'd felt slighted until she mentioned checking on him as well.

"Ironically, a week after I arrived home, Mr. Wilson sent a picture of Trip in front of their apartment, and another one three months later, with a note saying he wanted no attachments to Trip's past." Mom's voice catches. "It's like he knew I'd been there, even though I never rang the doorbell or even crossed the street."

"Your mom didn't feel she had a right to argue with Mr. Wilson about his decision," Daddy explains.

"I gave my babies away," Mom interjects, proceeding to weep like I've never seen her or anyone else in my whole life. I believe she'd saved these tears up from 1973. There were so many.

A box of Kleenex and quarter of a roll of paper towels later, Daddy looks at Mom. "Hardy?" he says, wiggling his thumb and forefinger.

She raises her silver eyebrows and nods, taking a deep breath as she brings her finger and thumb to her nose.

"It's a breathing technique that balances the right and left hemispheres of the brain," I tell Basil, who seems slightly puzzled.

Five cycles later, Mom is calm and glowing but still apologetic.

"Shame is so hard to shake," she says. "I am very sorry for any negative vibes I've caused either of you."

We are quick to comfort her, though neither of us will ever truly grasp how devastating it must've been for her to find out she was pregnant with triplets from a one night stand. She admits to feeling like a failure for putting her two sons up for adoption. "That's why I refused to have children with Daddy," she says, looking at me. "I couldn't take care of the ones I'd had, so ...."

Her voice trails off. She begins another cycle of deep breathing, closing off one nostril as she inhales, then the other as she exhales.

So she robbed herself and Daddy of kids of their own, I think to myself. I feel sorry for them but also selfishly happy that I had them to myself for so long.

☽

"Nuts and bolts," I say four hours later as Basil and I talk over coffee and brownies at the peninsula in my house. "Mom was young and scared." I bite into the slightly under-baked confection I'd made after Daddy left this morning. "She never let on. I would've never guessed. I swear."

"I haven't called my parents," Basil confesses. "I mean, what do I say? 'Hi Mom. Hello Dad. I found my birth mother. You know, the one you never told me about.'"

We both snort at the same time.

"How did we not know?" I ask, shaking my head. "We do look alike."

Same brown hair. We both have freckles. He's taller. I have brown eyes; his are green, but they are shaped the same, and we both have laugh lines etched at the outer edges. His face is a little more angular. But our smile is similar.

"We weren't paying attention," he says. "I mean, who goes out with someone and questions whether or not the other person is a sibling. Heck, I've heard people gravitate toward a partner they look like. It's familiar."

"Trip doesn't look as much like us," I say.

"Trip looks a lot like your … our … your mom," Basil stutters.

"I can't imagine how hard this must be for you."

"You don't know *your* dad either," Basil counters.

I start to argue but realize he's right. My biological father is out there somewhere. Mom didn't mention him in detail at all, and I'd had no inclination to ask. At first, I think this odd, then suddenly, this feeling of pride and love and gratitude rushes through me like water in a gutter after a strong summer storm. "My dad is right there," I say, pointing next door. "I have no desire to find the donor. That's all he is, really."

"What about Trip?" Basil counters, cutting a third brownie from the pan.

This subject has bothered me since I learned my other brother's name over voice mail. "Trip is a completely different story."

Basil drains his cup. "Let's find him."

I look into eyes that crinkle just like mine, look at a chin and mouth that are a whole lot more familiar without all that facial hair, feel a love flood my heart that is anything but romantic.

"Why not?" I offer.

"Let's," Basil says.

I finish off the last of my coffee, place my cup right next to his. "Let's."

☽

Basil shoves the last of our bags into a foot locker he has anchored to the floor at the back of the bus. He closes it and, suddenly, it's a chair. Affixed to the seat and wall are orange cushions from an old piece of furniture his mother let him tear up when he was outfitting his bus.

Evie, who has decided to join us on our adventure, climbs up through the back, passes the couch on her left, the table and benches on the right that are just beyond a sink, tiny counter, and cabinets below and above.

"This is so cool," she says, taking a load off just behind the driver's seat. I take the passenger's seat, Basil hops in behind the wheel, and, we're off.

The first few minutes, we talk only about the bus. It's safe. Nothing personal. No mention of the nervousness we are all feeling for one reason or another, yet the jittery energy fills the air.

"Where's the fridge?" Evie wants to know.

"In the far right cabinet beside the sink."

"Ahh."

Silence.

"The couch has a cushion underneath that slides out and locks in place. Makes a nice bed."

Evie has to go look. "And what's this?" She points to a long slender rectangular board latched to the wall just above the couch.

"A shelf if I need the space when I'm parked. It can also serve as a bed, you know, in case I have company." He tells us of a hiker who recently passed through Front Royal. "Met him at the Visitor's Center. His trail name's Baloo. He's hiking the AT and needed a break, so I offered for him to stay at the campground with me." Basil explains.

"You never said anything about this. That's so nice of you," I say.

"I can be nice when I want," Basil jokes, uncomfortable with the compliment.

"Wow ...." Evie says, stretching the word like a rubber band as she unlatches the board and lowers it.

"I attached a thin pad, but it's still kinda hard. Not as soft as the other. The windows are nice though. You can look out while you're falling asleep."

"Everything is so small and compact, yet it's just the right size all at once," Evie says, securing the board. "Can I sleep up there tonight?"

"Sure," Basil says, fiddling with the radio while we are sitting at a stop light.

"I thought we'd decided to get a room?" I mention. I like my small house, but I live there by myself. This space is hardly comfortable for three adults. I can't imagine trying to sleep here. We'd be shifting around like sand in an hourglass trying to make space for one another. Plus, I'd like a nice hot shower after traveling.

"Yeah, and it'd be pretty cramped in here with three of us," Basil says.

"You're right," Evie agrees as she takes her seat behind Basil again. Then she changes the subject. "I cannot believe I am doing this."

Here it is, I think to myself. *She's going to tell him.*

"It's been forever since I've taken a vacation." Evie looks out the window. I wonder what Basil's reaction will be when she tells him what she told me after she found out we were going to find Trip. But, instead of the confession I am expecting, she says, "I'll miss the kids." She is not talking about her biological children, Joe and Kate. She is talking about the kids she is responsible for in juvie. This is not, however, where I thought she was going with the conversation.

"You really love your job," Basil says, looking in the rearview mirror.

51

"We got a new kid in right before the end of my last shift. He's only in for a couple of days. Said he *wants* to be there, that he totally skipped school so he'd get thrown in juvie. Said he needs a break from all the crap at home."

"Wait. Kids go to jail for not going to school? That's crazy."

"Not when you've missed three years' worth."

"That happens?"

"Move enough times, need to take care of your drugged out parent enough times, do Dad's drugs yourself enough times ... the other side of the equal sign is juvie."

"Wow," Basil says. "Who knew?"

"Hey, where do we want to stop and eat?" I ask, completely meaning to interrupt Evie and Basil. If I don't, Evie will start worrying about the kids. We are still close enough to home for her to ask Basil to turn around. She did this to me once when we were on our way to the beach. She couldn't leave this girl, Trina, who'd tried to kill her mother's boyfriend. Evie said the jerk had it coming for doing some pretty horrible things to Trina.

"How did she end up in juvie if the mother's boyfriend was at fault?" I'd asked.

"Trina didn't say anything about the abuse until she'd been in juvie for two months," Evie explained. "I asked her about her favorite summer pastime, you know, tryin to get to know her, and, she burst into tears and told me everything."

Because Evie was the only one Trina had opened up to, Evie felt it was her responsibility to be there for the child. Needless to say, Puck and I went to the beach alone that summer. No way was I taking Fran.

"We'll find some diner along the way," Basil says, bringing me back to the present.

"That sounds good to me. How about you, Evie?"

She is checking her messages.

I reach back and take the phone, put it under my thigh.

"Hey, what are you doing?"

"Saving you from your big heart," I say and tell Basil about the beach.

His face softens into the sweetest smile. "Vi's right. Take a break. Have some fun."

"Oh, she's gonna have some fun all right." I turn and raise a brow at my best friend.

She screws up her face and jams her finger against her lips.

Why not? I mouth.

Evie rolls her baby blues.

Guess she's still feeling slightly embarrassed about the confession she made to me.

☽

We stop at a Sheetz two hours into the trip. Basil refills the tank while Evie and I use the restroom and grab coffee.

"Hey, Vi," she says as she rips the edge of two packets of sugar for Basil's coffee.

"Yeah?"

"I don't want Basil to know why I came along."

"Why not? I thought you said you were going to tell him?"

"I thought I was, but if it doesn't work out, if, you know, something is off, I don't want to seem like some desperate forty-something woman who couldn't make her dreams come true."

"Is that what you're calling it now? A dream?"

"Don't make fun."

I feel terrible for my friend and for making her feel like I was having a laugh at her expense. "I didn't mean it like that. Or, well, I guess I did." I put my arm around her. "I'm really sorry."

"Can we just let Basil think I want some time with you two?"

"That's not a lie," I tell her. "Who wouldn't want to spend a few days with Basil and me in a cramped bus?"

She grins, pours vanilla creamer until the coffee looks like tan milk. "Basil has the taste buds of a high school teenager," she says, changing the subject, a tactic I recognize well in my best friend.

I play along. "When it comes to coffee, yes."

☽

Before we left Front Royal, Basil had placed a rather sneaky call to find out where Trip lives. Because Basil insisted on phoning from a number that could not be traced back to us, we'd taken advantage of a sunny afternoon and walked the three blocks to the only pay telephone left in Front Royal, Virginia.

Rich Wilson answered on the third ring. "This is Rich," he'd said. "How can I help you?"

"Oh, well, uhm, I am trying to reach a, Trip Wilson, who also resides in New York." This was a longshot. We had no idea if Trip had remained close to his father. For all we knew he could live in Alaska.

"What's this about?"

"I am calling from the Red Cross to see if he'd like to schedule a time to give blood," Basil says into the mouthpiece.

"He's the other Wilson, the one just around the corner, 537 Enal. I'm on 535 Eel. You get us mixed up every time." Mr. Wilson provides a number that Basil repeats. I type it into my phone.

"Sorry to bother you," Basil says.

"Wait," I overhear. I am standing a breath away from Basil. "I'd like to give. Might I set up a time?"

Just then, Basil puts his hand over the phone and begins making crackling noises with his mouth. "Sir? You are breaking up, sir. I'll try back later." He hangs up.

"What, are you twelve?" Evie had asked.

"You're giving him too much credit," I'd said, rolling my eyes.

"We know where Trip Wilson lives now, don't we?"

"Yeah, and we have his number, too. Should we just call?" I ask.

"News like this is better in person," Basil argued.

"You're right," I'd agreed, feeling a tad inconsiderate.

"Guys?" Evie says, hesitantly, then stops.

"What?" Basil and I ask at the same time.

"Would you two mind if I tag along on this trip of yours?"

"Evie, that'd be great," I'd said, pleasantly surprised that she'd take a few days to go on a road trip with us.

"We'll have a blast," Basil said, slipping between the two of us and offering his elbows. We'd linked arms and headed back to my house where we made sandwiches and spent the rest of the evening planning our trip.

After Basil left, Evie told me the reason she wanted to go.

Needless to say, I was flabbergasted.

"You don't have to commit to anything," I'd advised as any best friend would, given the situation. "Go with us. If you want to follow through, follow through. If not, you had a great vacation with your best friend and her brother."

Evie had liked the sound of that.

☽

The plan is to take our time getting to New York. Rather than drive straight through, we've decided to make stops along the way and spend a night in a hotel before hitting the Big Apple to find our brother.

We stop at three farmer's markets all within the first leg of our journey. We buy fresh apples and Basil sells a portrait of a basket of fruit to the farmer's wife at stop number two.

Unlike me, my brother is quite the talker. I'm nice. Cordial. And I guess I'm not too shy, but Basil, he can talk the hind leg off a mule. Especially when it comes to strangers. He makes a connection within seconds. It's like he's always known everyone he sees. By the time we leave, he's on a first name basis and getting hugs goodbye. No wonder he doesn't have many paintings left to take back to his parents farm. He's a likeable talented guy.

After market three where Evie purchases a handmade bird feeder she falls in love with, I ask if they are ready for lunch. My stomach growls at the end of the question.

We decide on a diner called Mom and Pop's, a silver bullet looking building with a long counter lined with stools, and booths butted up against windows along the outer side. We slide into a booth with blue leather cushions. My side has a crack that pinches my thigh.

"Should've worn jeans," I say pulling at my shorts.

We peruse the menu, decide on our order, and wait patiently for the server, who is watching us from behind the counter, a curl of dyed white hair twisted around her finger. Her face is young looking, but we cannot determine her age. She's layered in makeup—white foundation and black eyeliner that she's drawn out far past her lids, making her look like a cat. Her lips are maroon.

Basil raises his hand in a wave. She rolls her eyes and grabs a pad and pen, then shuffles toward us, shoulders hunched, neck stretched forward like a goose.

"How are you?" Basil asks as she approaches.

"Whatever," she replies, sucking in her cheeks. This causes her bottom lip to protrude. Her eyes flutter closed. Her nostrils flare. It is apparent we are not welcome.

"I'll have a sweet tea and a BLT," Evie says politely to the closed eyes, killing our evil server with kindness.

The girl, whose name tag reads *Your Mom*, breathes deeply, opens her eyes, and tilts her head with just enough sass to let us know Evie's order has not been well received.

Your Mom's words are the same flat tone as that of someone playing a *c* over and over again on the clarinet. "We're out of the B and the T," she says.

"Oh, well, then, I guess I'll have the tuna salad."

"Egg salad's the special." I watch *Your Mom* scrawl the word *egg* on the pad.

"And you?" Without looking up, she points her pen in my direction.

"I'll have the club wrap. Spinach tortilla, please. And an iced tea."

"No iced tea. And no spinach tortillas."

It is my turn to point at the gentleman sitting at the counter. "He has one."

"Last one."

"Could ya check?"

She answers with an eye roll that leaves us wondering if her irises are gone for good.

I take a deep breath. This girl is grating my last nerve.

"I'll have the egg salad," Basil says, interrupting the rise in my blood pressure and urge to relieve it.

"Sure," she says, smiling like a prisoner who's stolen a cuff key from the jailer.

"I suppose I will too," I say, looking out the window. The view, a dumpster and a bicycle with a missing wheel, is far more aesthetically pleasing than our server.

She walks away, mumbling under her breath the entire way.

"She's a piece of work," Evie says quietly.

"I can't believe anyone would have her as an employee. Her attitude makes her ugly. I mean, she could be beautiful, but I don't think there's an ounce of kindness in her."

"Her parents probably own the diner," Evie offers. "I bet that's why she has a job."

Your Mom carries our drinks over, sets them in front of us, tipping each enough to slosh over the side. Next come our plates, with what looks to be pretty good food despite the poor service. I am starving. I cannot wait to bite into the egg salad I didn't want. Still, it looks like it should be in a *Taste of Home* magazine.

"I didn't order it, but I'm sure glad I got it," Evie says of the egg salad.

Basil nods in agreement, holds up his sandwich of which he's already had two bites. "Amazing. Totally worth the rude bitty of a server," he says a little too loudly.

I look toward the counter to see if *Your Mom* overheard and can't help but stare openly as she pulls a strand of hair from her scalp and pops it in her mouth. Evie and Basil are saying something about the texture of the mayonnaise; I nearly vomit. *Your Mom* sees me staring and smiles a wicked half smile, her heavily colored lips parting just enough for me to see her teeth open and close, chewing the snack. She pulls another strand, caresses it between thumb and forefinger before letting it drop onto a tray of empty glasses waiting to be filled.

I slap the table, get Basil and Evie's attention, and point.

Your Mom pulls out a few strands this time. She drops all but one. Her tongue snakes out like a chameleon's and snatches up the prize.

Evie gags. Basil drops his sandwich. Simultaneously, we stand. Evie and I grab our purses. I throw some money on the table as Basil spits into his napkin. We all but trip over one another as we head for the door. Behind us, a cackle erupts. It carries to the car.

☽

We decide to drive until we find an appealing exit, but, twenty miles go by and nothing strikes our fancy.

"I'm taking the next exit no matter what the restaurant and lodging signs advertise," Basil announces.

Turns out, the next exit does not even have a sign. Basil notices a tree with a small gold arrow and what looks like a narrow ramp.

"Where are we going?" Evie asks.

"I have no idea."

At the end of the narrow gravel road is a gold stop sign and a small sign with arrows that shoot both right and left.

"Secretsville, Pennsylvania," I read. "Never heard of it."

"Sounds like a ghost town," Basil says, flipping his blinker on to turn left.

"Or a place where they chop up the tourists and hide them in a cellar for next winter's stew." Evie can be incredibly morbid.

Secretsville must get its name from the twelve people who live there. Okay, so maybe I'm exaggerating, but I've seen maybe six people as we drive down Main Street. The others must be inside the lavish buildings that dot the landscape. Everything, and I do mean everything right down to the doorknobs and brick roads, is made of the fanciest materials money can buy.

We park in front of a breathtaking Inn that I know is going to be way out of even my price range, but we decide we have to go in and at least have a look.

"Then we'll search out some food and pick another hotel," Basil says.

"Everything I've seen looks just as posh."

"May have to head up the road."

At this, my stomach growls. "That apple wasn't enough," I say of the farmer's market snack I had to eat due to hair girl (my alternate name for *Your Mom*).

"How come we've never heard of Secretsville?" I wonder aloud as we climb the deep wide stairs (I count 82) to a concrete porch. White curtains are tied back between enormous pillars. You could fit a baby grand through the front doors.

Basil lifts the knocker and raps three times. "Because," Evie says, holding a finger to her lips, "It's a secret."

"Not the first time that joke has been told," replies the rather comfortably dressed man who answers the door. He looks out of place in his jeans and t-shirt. I was expecting a butler in a tux.

"Oh, uhm ..." Evie stumbles, not having meant to be overheard.

"Hi," I say, stepping forward. "My name's Violet. We thought we'd stop for a room, but it is unlikely that we'll be able to—"

"Free," the man says, turning his back and walking into a marble floored foyer the size of my house.

"Come again?" Basil asks.

The man turns, walks forward, tilts his head slightly and smiles. "You may stay for free." For the second time he turns and leaves.

We look at each other skeptically.

"Let's follow him," I say, and, together we walk the long hallway down which the man disappeared, opening and closing the doors of the library and a theater before finding him in what appears to be his office. He is hunched over a small roll top desk that's been shoved against a wall, just to the left of a floor-to-ceiling window. This is the smallest room we've seen so far. By the books stacked on chairs, and the clothes strewn over a coatrack, two half-empty coffee cups, and a smattering of odds and ends—tennis ball, 1950's radio out of which Elvis is rambling about blue suede shoes, toothbrush, toothpicks, and a medium-sized pair of lavender bunny slippers, the ears worn and gray at the ends, I assume this is his favorite room. It's certainly the most lived-in.

"Excuse me," I say to his back.

He scribbles furiously on a notepad. I am beginning to feel a tad like Charlie, only I don't have this guy's everlasting gobstopper and I don't believe he's going to offer for me to take over his factory.

Maybe this place isn't his. Maybe he only works here. This is what I'm thinking when he closes his laptop and turns to face us.

"We don't understand what you meant back there," I tell him.

"Sorry. I had to finish up an important letter," he says, ignoring my comment. He breathes in, his nostrils flaring, then exhales, reaching up to scratch a neatly trimmed salt and pepper beard. "Guess you're thinking you've gone through some portal, huh?"

Evie nods. "Something like that."

"Most people don't know we are here. Those who do happen by, usually drive right through. Too rich, too clean, too small, too whatever, they think. That's my guess, anyway. Those who do park and engage in conversation, end up staying for a time. Some stay forever. Those who leave, assure us they will never tell a soul they've been here."

"Why?" I ask.

"You'll see," he promises, then holds out his hand. "My name is Grayson. Grayson Weir."

We take turns introducing ourselves.

"Hungry?" he asks.

"Famished," I say.

He ushers us back to the front door and opens it.

"I will take you to the best restaurant in town. The only restaurant, in fact."

We follow him back outside and down the steps.

"Just there." He points to the restaurant that is situated at an angle to the right of the cul-de-sac. A seasonal garden, dotted with lovely wildflowers throughout, spills onto the street. Every color of the rainbow is represented. I truly feel as if I am in another world.

We pass store after store, each sign beginning with *Secretsville* followed by the service offered—hardware, salon, clothing, grocery.

Each building is magnificent. Some are red brick, some white. The pillars are stunning with their ornately sculpted molding—curlicues and squares, and designs that remind me of doodle pages, all intricately connected, a story in each and every piece. Each building has a deep porch that stretches from corner to corner, some wrap around. The stairs are wide enough to take two steps on each, and there are lots of them, with ramps on either side. "Just in case," Grayson explains. "Haven't needed them yet, but one never knows."

The scent of smoked meat and a sugary dessert overwhelms our senses the closer we get to the restaurant. It is warm outside, so the patio seating is full as is the dining room. *So, more than a handful of people reside here, after all.*

"Some come on a specific night, others every day. Just depends," Grayson says of the crowd. "Most are here on this beautiful evening," he concludes, shaking hands or waving as he leads us to a table in the center marked with an engraved plate that reads *Guests*. The restaurant chatter has quieted noticeably. Everyone must be wondering who we are. Grayson pulls out a chair for myself and then Evie, makes sure we are comfortable, then announces our names.

"And these wonderful people," he says, motioning to everyone inside and outside of the restaurant, "are most of the Secretsville community."

We receive a mix of hello's and nice to meet you's and then everyone returns to their meal.

"They won't overwhelm you," Grayson says, taking a seat at our table. "We're all pretty laid back here."

Dinner is delicious and not just because I am famished. I especially love the blackberry cobbler. The meal is so good, in fact, that I do not even lose my appetite when I find a long white hair clinging to my shirt sleeve.

When it is time to leave, I pull out my credit card and look for a place to pay, as do Basil and Evie. But, when Basil asks for the bill, the server explains our meal is free.

"You may leave a donation, if you like," he says, when we insist. He points to a jar on the bar.

I don't usually pay with cash, so I am not carrying much. Recalling that Grayson has also said our lodging is free, I can only assume the same donation rule applies. I make a mental note to ask after the ATM as I make my way to the jar to drop in a twenty. I reserve another twenty for the room just in case there is no ATM. Everything about this place is surreal; at this point, I'm not counting on the conveniences of today's technology.

Outside, some people are mingling. They introduce themselves and the place of business they are associated with, make small talk about the weather, and welcome us to the town.

"Everything and everyone is incredible. This place is too good to be true," Basil whispers in my ear.

"Only it's not," Grayson replies, clapping a gentleman on the shoulder and wishing him a good evening before returning his attention to Basil. "Sorry, you're whisper is loud. Secretsville is only too good to be true because much of society doesn't function as we do."

I find myself interested in more of an explanation than Grayson has given; Evie and Basil, on the other hand, look as if they just want a good night's sleep.

We make our way back to the Inn, stopping here and there to window shop.

"Stay in any room you like on the second floor, except the third on the left. That's my room. All the others are vacant," Grayson says as we enter the foyer.

Evie and Basil thank our host and start up the stairs. I tell them I'll catch up.

"Do you mind if I stay down here for a while?"

"Not at all. I was hoping for your company, actually."

Grayson shows me to the verandah. We sit side by side on a swing. I slip off my flops and push off with my big toe, setting in motion a conversation that lasts into the wee hours of the morning. As we talk, I watch the sun sink behind the mountains, wishing that God would stretch out the night like he did for Odysseus and Penelope. I realize I've never felt so comfortable talking to anyone.

He gives me a morsel about every resident from the grocer who hums his hello if you happen by him when he's retrieving his paper first thing in the morning, "because he's oil pulling," Grayson explains, to the couple who wear matching outfits to church every Sunday.

"I know people like this in the real world," I say. "But you are right. This place is different. Why do you think that is?"

"We are blessed with peace. Every one of us. Not just a few. All. We are positive thinking, peaceful people. Period. That's the secret. We do not know negative in Secretsville."

I contemplate this and think how nice it must be. Zero negative. I like it.

My thoughts drift until my curiosity fixes on a nugget of information it wants to know.

"What do you do for a living?" I ask.

"I sell socks," he states matter-of-factly.

"You sell socks?"

Grayson nods and repeats, "I sell socks."

I wait for him to elaborate. He details his online business that is successful, he claims, because of the giving component. "For every pair I sell, one pair is given away to a person of the buyer's choice."

"So they choose the recipient themselves?"

"Yep."

"Why not make it so they have to give to someone in need?"

"Too complicated. I do my part in making the offer. It's up to the buyer to do what they want."

"What makes your socks better than everyone else's?"

"I love what I do."

"What part?"

"All of it. Choosing the designs, making sure they are durable, soft, what I'd want for myself."

"Why socks?"

"Why not?"

We swing in silence for a time. I am well aware of the give and take of conversation, that it is my turn to share. I take a deep breath, push against the porch floor with a little more gusto, swinging us faster, more in time with my heartrate, and tell Grayson what everyone in Front Royal has known from the moment I returned to Robinson's Store where I'd purchased the ticket, to see how, exactly, I was to collect my winnings.

"I remember Mom being on the phone with a reporter from the Northern Virginia Daily when I came home with a paper upon which was written ***Winner's Guide***. I'd left the store literally two minutes before. An article appeared in the morning paper, and, after, I had friends galore. I'd been popular enough. My parents are good people, as am I. We are well-liked. But Lord have mercy, after I hit the jackpot, everyone in town wanted to claim the Shines' as their best friends. Surprisingly, it wasn't to get to my money. They all just wanted bragging rights. They wanted to be able to say they knew the teenager who won the lottery.

"The lottery, huh?"

"Yep."

"What do you think you'd have done if you hadn't won all that money?"

"I don't know. Maybe work in a library. I love books."

"Hmm. What about your friends? Basil and ... Evie, is it?"

I nod.

"What do they do?" he asks. Before I can answer, he adds, "And ... if you don't mind my asking, where are you headed?"

Grayson doesn't realize the sizeable floodgate he's unlatched.

I talk until my throat hurts, through three glasses of sweet tea, a drink normally unknown the further north one travels. I tell him everything, some stuff I didn't even know I was feeling. Like, what if Basil decides he doesn't want his parents to know about me? What if he does? What if Trip is a jerk? What if they want a relationship with my mother who is actually their mother too? What if I don't want to share?

When I finish, I take a cleansing breath. "Sorry for dumping on you like that."

"You have no reason to apologize."

"I've talked your ear off."

He grabs both lobes. "They are still right here."

"Tell me about you," I say, briefly resting my hand on his arm. He feels … strong.

"I have. I sell socks. Not much else to tell."

"Not much else to tell? Come on," I say, sitting taller and waving my hand in a half circle. "This place is a fantasy land. While I admit, your sock business is truly fascinating, I know there's more. I've told you my life story. Now, I want to know all of yours."

"You really want to know?"

"I really want to know."

"I'm a regular guy who sells socks for a living. I have one brother and one sister. You met them at the restaurant."

"How do you figure into *this* place? You know, Secretsville? Do you run the Inn? Do you own the town?"

"No one owns the town, but I guess you could say I run it. I'm the oldest in the family, so the duty fell to me."

"Are all the people here family?"

"Connected in some way, but no, not all family. But, we have a few randoms who stopped here and never left."

"Sounds like you do more than sell socks."

He shrugs. "Maybe."

Unlike me, who spilled my guts, Grayson is more reserved.

"Do you have any hobbies?"

"I like to hike and garden."

"I like to think I like to garden, but really, I like the idea of it," I admit.

Grayson chuckles.

"So, you created the garden at the end of the road?"

"That's my biggest gardening project, yes. But, I help people at their homes, too. If you hang around long enough tomorrow, I'll show you the gardens in the village."

"The village." I repeat, knowing already that I'm gonna love it.

Grayson grows quiet. I can almost see him thinking. His brown eyes look off into the darkness, and his mouth draws together like a purse that's been closed.

"Something wrong?" I ask.

He looks at me as if I've appeared out of nowhere. "Just considering."

His answer lands between us, a smoke signal that dissipates when I lay my hand on his. "Tell me," I urge.

And he does. He informs me that he's never really talked with an outsider like this. That he wishes I didn't have to leave.

Oddly enough, I feel the same way. I could spend eons with Grayson. In a few short hours I've learned that this man is the butter to my fly. On the heels of that realization, however, a rush of shame fills me up. I'm like a broken bottle with a message inside that's been ruined in the water. The focus of this trip is not as clear. I should be wanting to find my brother, but instead, I want to stay here in this place that seems to be a page torn from a book, a cross between fantasy and a time long ago.

My feelings are a mess, and it scares me. I look at my Fitbit for the time. "Oh my goodness. It is nearly three in the morning." I slip my feet into my flip flops, stand up and stretch. "I better head to bed."

"I didn't mean to frighten you."

I sit down again, turn to face him. "You didn't frighten me, Grayson. The fact that I feel the same way is what's causing my stomach to feel like there's a butterfly parade going on inside of me.

Grayson wrinkles his brow.

"I'm scared of how I feel. I've spent a few hours with you and all of a sudden I want to postpone looking for my brother to spend more time with you."

Grayson takes my hand, gently turns my palm upward, and places a kiss right in the center.

"I'm not going anywhere. You go find your brother. I'll be here if you want to come back."

He stands, pulls me to my feet, kisses my cheek. "Goodnight, Violet Shine."

"Goodnight."

☽

I walk upstairs alone, avoiding the two rooms that have birdcages just outside the door, each with a canary perched on a swing, *the sign for occupied*, I read on a framed parchment in the hall entrance. We are the only guests, so I assume correctly that the two occupied rooms belong to my brother and best friend. I choose the next available room, move the pineapple inside as the parchment instructed, and replace it with the canary that greets me cheerily from a stand just inside the doorway.

"You're a cutie," I say, leaving him in the hall with his friends.

Inside, I turn on the light and sigh over the enormous four poster bed just waiting for me to tug down the satin sheets and climb in. I don't care that I've left my stuff in the car and will have to sleep in my t-shirt. I'm tired and that bed is so darn inviting.

I fold back the bedding and place one knee on the most comfortable mattress I've ever touched, sleep only seconds away. I've barely settled into the cushiony heaven, when I hear a noise—*Laughter maybe? More like crooning*—on the balcony. My curiosity gets the best of me. I pad across the plush carpet to the French doors and pull back the curtains. I am stunned at what I see.

Under the moonlight, wine glasses forgotten on a wrought iron table, are Basil and Evie slow dancing to a song my brother is singing quite well. *Oh my darlin you look wonderful …*

The last word he sings too softly for me to hear.

"Oh my stars," I whisper, wondering how in the world Evie is going to get herself out of this predicament, and hoping that my brother doesn't get his heart broken.

)

At noon, I make my way downstairs and find Grayson in his "office." He is, once again, typing furiously on his laptop. I wait a moment, then clear my throat.

"We're heading out," I say.

Another minute goes by before he clicks send and turns to acknowledge me. *So, our goodbye will mimic our hello*, I think to myself. Only, my feelings now are much different from the simple curiosity I'd felt less than twenty-four hours ago.

"Sorry," he begins, lifting a hand to massage the back of his neck.

I wave his apology away. "I know. You had to finish."

"A bit of a completest." He looks up at me, his hand still on the nape of his neck.

"So I've learned."

Grayson smiles, drops his hand, and, in one step, clears the space between us. He kisses me like I've never been kissed before. Not skilled, necessarily, but meaningful, like he's allowing me to taste a piece of his soul.

"Say you'll come back and stay," Grayson whispers, his lips a breath away from mine.

I step back. Stay sounds so … permanent. "I can come *visit*," I offer. "And maybe you can visit me?"

Grayson bristles and does not respond. It seems he's too busy building a wall.

"Of course, if you don't want to visit …." I don't finish. I'm not sure how to conclude this statement.

He starts to answer, but is interrupted by Evie and Basil.

"Ready?" Basil asks.

I take another step back and turn away from Grayson. "Yeah. Sure," I manage.

"Let me walk you out."

I smile hesitantly at Grayson, hoping Evie and Basil don't have a clue, but something tells me they are onto us much like we are onto them. After the beautiful morning the four of us spent together, any onlooker would think we are two very in love couples out to breakfast and sightseeing.

At the bus, Grayson extends a hand to Basil, gives Evie and awkward hug, before wrapping his arms around me. "Please come back."

I am not ready to divulge my feelings to Evie who is waiting to take the back seat.

"Go ahead and take the front" I tell her.

I wait for her to close the door, for Basil to fire the engine.

Safe from being overheard, I ask, "Will you come see me?"

Immediately, Grayson seems distant, just like he had in the office. "Violet, I really like you. In fact, I've never liked anyone like I like you. And, I believe you feel the same."

"Silly as it sounds, yes, I do."

"In less than a day, I believe I've found my forever person, the woman I want to spend the rest of my life with."

I shrug. "This is crazy, huh?"

"But …."

I tilt my head, trying to get him to look me in the eye. "But?"

"But, I have everything I need right here."

"What's that supposed to mean?"

"I've built my life here."

"You just said you want to be with me but that you have everything you need here." I pause. "I'm not here." I pause again, then add, "I'm confused."

"That came out wrong. I want to be with you. My happily ever after is you in Secretsville with me."

My emotions are doing somersaults in my stomach.

"Well, I can't just up and leave my own home and family. I have a life, too, you know. "

"Yeah," he says, suddenly interested in picking nonexistent lint off his shirt.

"Guess this is goodbye," I say and turn to leave.

I open the bus door and climb inside. When I look out the window, Grayson manages a half-smile, lifts his hand and waves.

I look away, lean between the seats and say to Basil and Evie, "Let's blow this popsicle stand."

)

"What just happened back there?" Evie asks as we pull onto the interstate.

"I don't know," I say and mean it. I really don't know what just happened. Grayson didn't mention being a town hermit. In fact, he'd demonstrated the exact opposite. He told me about business trips he takes, and vacations. Yet, he doesn't want to leave his precious town to come see me. I don't get it. *Oh well*, I think to myself, grateful to have put so little time into a relationship that clearly will never work. Trouble is, my heart is in my stomach, and all I can think about is the touch of his hand as he led me through the cobbled streets of the village, excited, he said, to see Secretsville through my eyes.

"I think you guys are made for each other." Evie's words come out in a childish sing-song fashion that makes me angry.

"How about we talk about what's going on with you and Basil? You want to talk about that?" I snap.

Evie faces forward; Basil fiddles with the radio.

"Okay then. I don't want to talk about Grayson. He's a nice man. We had a nice evening talking. That's it."

Just then, my phone dings. A text. I look down and see Grayson's name. How could I have forgotten? We'd exchanged numbers the night before.

I'm a schmuck.

--Yes, you are, I respond.

Forgive me?

--Tell me why you don't want to come see me.

It's not that.

--Then, what?

Long story.

--Oh yeah?

I'll work on it.

--Don't strain yourself.

I turn off my phone. I refuse to get my feelings hurt again.

☽

I remove myself to the back of the bus, hoping a few feet of space will do us all some good. The mattress on the pull out couch is more comfortable than I expect, yet I do not fall asleep. Instead, I review the morning that somehow feels like ten years ago.

I'd wakened rested and joy-filled. I hurried to search out Grayson, who was hard at work in the kitchen preparing a breakfast fit for royalty. Eggs, bacon, sausage, biscuits, gravy, pancakes, fruit with yogurt dip.

"We'll never be able to eat all of this," I'd said, sipping a fancy coffee he'd prepared. It had a hint of chocolate in the aftertaste.

Grayson swung a towel over his shoulder. "Don't worry. It won't go to waste. I'll drop any leftovers by the restaurant." He stole a glance my way, smiled nervously.

"I didn't mean to ...." I trailed off. I didn't know what I was going to say, really. I could tell I hadn't offended him, yet he was having difficulty being around me.

"Listen, I ... I ...." Grayson turned the burner back and faced me. "I really really like you."

My heart felt full to bursting.

"I really really like you too."

Grayson took my hands. "I've known you for less than a day, but it feels like—"

"You've known me forever," I finished for him. "I've been thinking the same about you."

"I want you to—"

"Good morning," Evie and Basil called from the entryway.

I spun around, a cat caught eating the canary. I was not ready to tell them about what was going on, but by Evie's raised brow and Basil's grin, I was certain they already knew. I tilted my head, screwed up my lips and squinted. Evie knew I meant for her to keep quiet, but Basil blurted, "What's that look for?" I was mortified. I had to wait a moment before I turned back to Grayson.

"Nothing, Basil," I said, stretching out the end of his name like a rubber band, that, if handy, I'd love to shoot at him.

"Breakfast," Grayson said. I turned back to him and smiled when he winked. All I could think was how long it'd been since someone had read my thoughts. He knew I wasn't ready to tell them anything, and he was saving me.

We talked about the weather, the trip, how much longer it'd take to get to New York. And we talked about the birds.

"Who takes care of them when the rooms are vacant?" Evie asked.

"Me. The Inn is my job in Secretsville."

"Who chose to have birds instead of occupied signs?" Basil wants to know.

"I did."

"Why?" I asked.

Grayson grins. "Why not?"

After breakfast on the back patio, we'd packaged the leftovers to take to the restaurant on our way to the village. As amazing as Main Street was, the village was even more wonderful, but in a much different way.

While Main Street was impressive and overstated, grand and upscale, the village was full of modest homes that reminded me of hobbit houses. Most had cedar shakes and tin roofs, a few were brick or white stucco. All had porches and sunrooms. It was the circular doors that reminded me most of hobbit houses. That and the gardens. Every yard was an explosion of color.

"You did all of this, didn't you?" I'd asked.

"I helped," he said, but I knew this was an understatement. "Working with nature is my passion," he'd admitted as he picked the brown leaves from the stem of a purple blue flower that seemed a cross between a rose and a petunia. "But the homeowners work just as hard as I do."

"Gardens and socks," I'd said, smiling at this unique man I knew God had created just for me.

"Weird, huh?"

"Yes it is," I agreed then added, "The most fantastic combination of wonderful I could ever imagine."

Then everything went straight downhill. Only, I didn't know that's where it was going. I went back to the room at the Inn, left an IOU in an envelope on the dresser (because there's no such thing as an ATM in Secretsville), said goodbye to the bird, and headed to the office. That's when everything changed.

Now, here I am trying to make sense of it all. We admitted our feelings, said we wanted to be together, then Grayson changed it all. Well, not all. But he gave me an ultimatum. If I want to be with him, it'll have to be in Secretsville. He made it clear he is not willing to come to me. I feel like the woman in that Santa Claus movie with Tim Allan. If she wants him, she has to leave everything behind and move to the North Pole. I sigh, throw an arm over my eyes. *What? Is Grayson the sock Santa?*

We stop about twenty minutes outside of our destination because Evie has to use the bathroom. And we are hungry. Basil chooses a hole-in-the-wall sub shop. I am waiting for *Your Mom* to pop up from behind the counter, but she doesn't. Instead, a nice man tells us to sit wherever we like. I leave my purse with Basil and follow Evie to the bathroom where I know we will have a few minutes to talk privately.

I am waiting for her when she comes out of the stall.

"Look, sorry about earlier. I was just ... fed up." Before she can ask for details, I rush into a new topic, choosing to exchange my sour mood for a good one. I am not about to let a man ruin this trip. "What's going on between you and Basil?" I ask, arms folded, a gleam in my eye.

"I could ask the same about you and Grayson," she says, searching my eyes in the reflection of the mirror as she washes her hands.

"Have you told him why you came with us?"

"No," Evie says, shaking off the excess water into the sink.

"Are you gonna?"

Evie changes the subject. "What *is* going on between you and Grayson?"

"Nothing." I squash the urge to return to a bad mood.

Evie cocks an eyebrow, shifts so her hip rests against the sink. She is not going to let me avoid the question.

"I mean, I thought ... but then ... he doesn't want to leave Secretsville. Says he has all he needs there."

Evie frowns. "But you two look like you're meant for each other." She folds her arms across her chest. "I was thinking how surreal it is for the both of us to fall in lo…."

Evie catches herself, but it's too late.

"You love Basil?"

Her chin juts forward. "What if I do?"

I smile. "I think it's great. But you need to tell him why you came with us."

"Why? I can go do what I have to do, and he'll never know. Why rock the boat when it's only started sailing?"

"I think your boat's starting with water in it and you need to dock and dump before setting out for deep sea."

"I think we better go find Basil before he starts thinking we fell in."

At the door she pauses. "Basil doesn't care that you know about us."

I reach around her and pull the door. "Apparently, Grayson doesn't care at all."

☽

The ride is far less stressful since the bathroom talk. The laundry has been aired, so to speak. Well, most of it has, anyway. If Evie would tell Basil what I believe is important for him to know, I'd feel much better. But, she is unwilling, and it isn't my place to tell him, so I talk about Grayson instead.

"Everything was perfect," I tell them. "We talked all evening. I've never felt so comfortable with someone."

"What about me?" Basil asks, chuckling.

"Look," I say, meeting his gaze in the rearview mirror as I've permanently demoted myself to the back seat.

"That shenanigans is more than weird now. I can't even think about it."

"Did you and Grayson exchange favorite colors?" Evie asks. She knows this is my gauge as to how serious the relationship is.

I think back and realize that we did not talk at all about favorite colors. The little bit of hope that'd remained in my heart, went dark as night.

When I don't respond, Evie turns and gives me her *youpoorthing* face.

"Oh, stop," I say, waving her off. "It's fine. It was a one-time thing. Not even a thing. A conversation. A way to pass time." I look out the window to hide the expression on my face that, I am certain, is a dead giveaway. "It was nothing," I say, thinking of the way he kissed me goodbye, the safe, warm, complete way it made me feel. Something I am not willing to discuss with anyone.

Thankfully, Basil turns up the radio and sings along. *We've got the beat, we've got the beat, we've got the beat, yeah. We've got the beat.*

☽

Nosilla is easier to find than Mom said it would be. It's grown from a sliver to a decent sized wedge since Mom was here all those years ago. We find the Hotel Nekcihc, situated on the corner of Eldoon and Puos. The suite is beautiful. I spend some time on the balcony, queen of the seventh story, surveying the land. Everyone has somewhere to go. The energy hums and thumps to a beat only a true city girl could love: I am not that girl. I see a man miming, caged in an invisible box of his own making; a fountain of three dogs, each spewing water out of its mouth; a ballerina pirouetting across the street; cars eating one another's exhaust for dinner; and more people filling the maze of buildings than I've ever seen in any one place.

We've decided to wait until tomorrow to meet Trip. Hopefully, because it is Sunday, he will be home.

I sleep in fits and starts. Evie curls up next to me, flops an arm over my middle, and, I could swear calls me Basil. In the other bed, arms and legs splayed across the full span of the queen is Basil, the moon bright enough to show the sweet smile of a restful sleep. Carefully, I remove Evie's arm, grab my phone, and make my way to the balcony.

The breeze is warm. I contemplate the smell of this city, a combination of man-made-ness, homelessness, and hope, and compare it to home where it smells of earth and peace and contentment. I take a quick scroll through Facebook before checking the notifications, putting off the inevitable, which is finding out if one of the messages is from Grayson.

Mom left a voicemail.

There's a text from Evie from earlier, when I'd gotten testy before going to the back of the van.

Hope everything is okay. Let me know if there's anything I can do. She followed the message with her bitmoji, a short blonde replica of herself in jeans and a green t-shirt, sporting a smile and holding a heart that says *Love U.*

I laugh to myself and send a response that she will see in the morning: My own Bitmoji in jeans and a red zip-up hoodie, mouth slightly frowning, shoulders a bit droopy, with a word bubble that says, *Forgive Me?* even though she already has.

Finally, I check the last notification. My heartbeat quickens when I see it is from Grayson. He has sent another apology. *I'm sorry.*

These two words do not fix anything for me. The trouble is, I have no idea why Grayson is apologizing. Is it for the way he left things? Has he rethought what he said? Does he now want to meet me halfway in this relationship that's barely been given a chance? Or, is he sorry that he can't do his part? That he wants me to give up everything so he can remain comfortable in Secretsville? I type a text: *What do you mean?* then delete it. I settle for a question mark and hit send.

I stretch, roll my head from left to right attempting to relieve the tension in my neck, then look over the balcony and find that, even in the dark, it appears to be daytime in New York. Well-lit. People everywhere. I yawn for them, look back into the room and see Evie now splayed in much the same fashion as Basil. "Good luck getting any sleep if y'all get together," I murmur. I am tired, but have no desire to try and wrestle Evie to her side of the bed. Since it is warm, I decide to grab my pillow and blanket and sleep under the smog. No stars can be seen twinkling here.

I fall asleep to distant music and the hum of traffic and voices, shrieks and sirens. I wake up dreaming a dentist is shining a light in my eyes, when, in reality, it is the sun.

"Rise and shine," I hear, the brightness suddenly disappearing. I open my eyes and find the shade is Basil's face blocking the sun.

Surprisingly, I am well-rested. I stretch, sit up, scratch my head, and smile. "Today's the day."

"Yep."

Evie joins us on the balcony. She's juggling three mugs of coffee room service dropped off at her request. We sit and sip, watching the throng below us thrive.

"It never dies," I say of the energy. "Just ebbs and flows."

"Mmmm," Basil agrees mid-sip. "More flowing than ebbing though."

"Agreed."

A low roar can be heard over the noise below.

Basil frowns and looks down at his stomach. "I suppose you know I'm hungry now."

Evie gives him a playful slap on the shoulder. "Why didn't you say something?" She gets up; Basil and I remain seated. Evie throws her arms out, her oversized nightshirt making her look a little like a kite. "Well, what are y'all waiting for? Let's go downstairs and get something to eat."

I think of the time it's going to take to get myself presentable and offer an alternative. "How 'bout we call room service for breakfast, too?"

Evie rolls her eyes and smacks herself on the forehead. "Why didn't I think to order breakfast? Now they're going to think I don't value their time."

Another of Evie's quirks is worrying about what others think. Though Basil has only known her for a short while, he's picked up on this.

"How 'bout I go get our breakfast. That way no one will know you secretly love to overwork hotel staff?" he teases, then, in his best British accent adds, "I need to stretch my legs anyway. You girls can relax and ..." Basil falters momentarily, "and do whatever ladies do when the men aren't around."

"You sound like a British Rastafarian," Evie says, laughing.

I can't help but laugh, too.

Basil grins, then bows and lets himself out.

The door is closed less than five seconds when I begin firing questions at a retreating Evie.

"Well?" I begin.

Evie points to the bathroom. "Shower," she manages.

"Oh no you don't." I'm out of my chair in a heartbeat. "When, Evie? When are you going to tell him?"

Evie runs a hand through her tousled blond bob. "Today," she answers. "I guess."

"What do you mean, you guess? You have to tell him, Evie. It's not fair for him to think everything's hunky dory."

Evie shifts her weight onto her left hip and fixes her fist at her waist. "Everything *is* hunky dory, Vi. As soon as I go have a little meeting, it's all gonna be like nothing was ever going on."

"I don't know," I tell her. "I feel like something's not okay."

"You're paranoid."

"I don't want to see my best friend or my brother get hurt. I'm not used to being stuck in the middle of a family *thing*."

Evie nods. "If it's that important to you, I'll be sure and tell him."

"Before you go do it?"

Evie nods. "Before I go do it."

"Go do what?" Basil asks, kicking the door closed and turning to reveal three sacks with golden arches.

"What happened to getting something from downstairs?" I ask, changing the subject. I do not want to be a part of the conversation that will ensue once Evie fesses up.

"Breakfast is over."

I look at my wrist and realize my Fitbit is dead. "Crap."

"No, I did not get crap. I got pancakes and sausage. From McDonalds. Only, I never stepped inside the restaurant."

He takes the bags out on the balcony. "Fortunately for us, a lovely couple saw me standing on the sidewalk looking rather out of sorts as I was trying to determine what to do. Add my attire," he looks at himself, which begs we take a gander, "and, you've got the look of ...."

He trails off, leaving us to figure out what's happened.

I pull my lips under my teeth to keep from laughing. "You're telling us you acquired that food because some poor couple thought—"

"Well, I wouldn't call them poor," Basil corrects, flashing his dimples. "They did give us their breakfast."

"Wait." Evie has just put two and two together. "They thought you were homeless?"

Basil nods.

"And you didn't correct them?"

"They wouldn't listen. I tried to tell them my shoes are in my room. They told me I shouldn't be embarrassed. The man was ready to give me his shirt, but I took off before he could get it over his head."

The shirt Basil is wearing *has* seen better days. It's splattered with all sorts of paints and oils.

"Why didn't you leave the food?"

"They'd handed it to me, and, well ...." His eyes are wide as a toddler trying to get out of timeout for coloring on the wall. "The line at McDonald's is out the freaking door."

The three of us stand there in silence for a moment. Evie laughs first. Basil and I follow. We laugh until our sides ache, until the pancakes have to be reheated in the microwave.

☽

"I think I'm gonna take a walk while you two are getting ready," I say, slipping into my shoes. "I need some exercise."

"Back by 11:30?" Basil asks, checking his phone.

I retrieve my Fitbit from its charger. "Sure thing."

I say goodbye, raise my eyebrows at Evie who is standing behind Basil, eyes squinting, lips screwed up, shooing me along.

Outside, I stop on the sidewalk, trying to decide which way I want to go. People flow around me like water around a rock. A girl in flannel, baseball cap turned backwards, acknowledges me with a smile. As she passes I hear her say into her phone something about tourists being in the way.

I decide to go right with the flow of the other bodies, let them sweep me away. Most everyone moves fast here, but not all. The homeless sit on the curb or a bench or hang out in alleys, calling out, a cap or a cup or a pocket ready to be filled. Love also takes its time. Couples are seated outdoors, holding hands across the table, while sipping lattes and soaking up conversation like quicker-picker-uppers. Everyone else is full tilt.

Five blocks later, I choose a coffee shop to duck into—a haven from which to watch the madness up close without being swallowed.

I sit alone at the only remaining table until Flannel Girl approaches and asks if the seat next to me is taken. I've never been asked to share a table with a stranger, but it's okay with me.

"You visiting?" she asks.

I nod. "Guess you could tell back there."

Her cheeks turn red. "You heard?"

"Yeah," I say and grin.

"Don't worry. You were trying to find your way. Sorry if I hurt your feelings. I was being ...."

"Accurate," I finish before she can berate herself. "It's okay. Really."

I don't catch the name the barista calls from behind the counter.

"That's me," Flannel girl says, reaching down to tighten the shoelaces on a pair of chucks that have clearly walked too many miles in this city. She stands to leave. "There's a pizza place three blocks back. If you're staying a while, you should try it."

"Thanks. I'll do that."

"Don't linger in the people traffic," she says, smiling. "Someone might mistake you for a tourist."

"Thanks for the advice."

"Have a nice day."

I sit for a few more minutes, sipping coffee and watching. It's warming up nicely. I'm no longer sorry I wore shorts and a tee. The poor guy across the street has to be roasting. It is probably close to seventy-five degrees, yet he is layered in black. A shirt sticking out beneath a heavy hoodie. A toboggan covering long hair that clings to his neck. Glasses that cover half his face. All I can think is, *he's hiding*. Either that, or he's attempting to sweat himself into oblivion.

I listen as a short round-faced woman with orange hair, big round brown eyes, and an even bigger rounder chest and derriere, asks a policeman if he'll help her find her boyfriend.

"What's your name?" he asks, very serious-like, taking out a pad and pen.

"Aliya," she answers. "Aliya Lot."

"How long's your boyfriend been missing?"

"Years."

"What is his name?"

"I can't tell you that," she says.

"Why not?"

"Because. If his wife finds out I'm lookin for him, she might get mad. She's a monster of a thing. She'd squash me dead."

"First of all, if you don't tell me his name, I can't help you. Second of all, if he's married, you shouldn't be looking for him anyway."

"What'll I do?" she asks.

"You might try finding a new boyfriend," the policeman offers.

"You single?" she asks, tilting her head to her shoulder and wiggling her brows. When she smiles, her lips disappear.

The police officer flips his blank pad closed and pockets his pen.

"Are you in any danger, ma'am?

"No. I don't think so. Unless … do you think Shianne knows I'm looking for Drake?" She claps her hand over her mouth. "I didn't mean to say his name."

"Pardon me, ma'am," the policeman says, then tips his hat and moves along before Aliya can make any more moves. I find this exchange extremely entertaining until she turns and makes direct eye contact with me. "I need to find a man," she says, making her way toward me.

I take one last swig of my coffee, toss the cup and hightail it outta there before Ms. Lot can clamber over the chain and share her woes.

My walk back to the hotel is just as amusing as Aliya Lot and the policeman. I see a woman dressed in white with black polka dots, a matching Dalmatian at her side. She is talking on a phone and smoking a cigarette out of one of those long skinny stick things. I watch a runner get hit by a car. He smacks the hood, yells, "Watch where you're going," and takes off, clearly unharmed and unaffected by the whole ordeal. One block later, I see a different runner, same ordeal. Also unfazed. I pass the pizza shop Flannel Girl mentioned, step in a wad of gum, pet two dogs at a crosswalk, decline when their owner offers me a tic tac. Once I'm out of his line of vision, I hold my hand in front of my face and blow. Coffee breath. I make a mental note to brush my teeth when I reach the hotel room.

My breath, however, quickly becomes the last of my worries when I open the door to find Basil and Evie in a lip lock that'd make a harlot flush.

I clear my throat, hoping to break the seal. Thankfully, it does.

Evie is beaming. "It's official. Basil and I have discussed what's been going on between us these last couple of days and ..." She pauses for, I can only imagine, the dramatic effect. "We have decided to make it official. We're a couple." She then moves out of Basil's line of vision and runs a finger across her lips, a warning.

"Think we make a good couple?" Basil asks, pulling Evie close.

"I think … I think … you two look great together," I manage. And they do. Look great together. But I know Evie has to leave soon, and it is most apparent that she has not filled Basil in on where she is going.

Evie says, "I'm going to get dressed and do some sightseeing while y'all go meet Trip."

Basil kisses her cheek, places a hand at the nape of her neck, trying out his new boundaries. "Why not come with us?" he asks, looking from her to me. "That'd be okay, wouldn't it? You wouldn't mind, would you?"

Evie begins fidgeting with the belt on her robe. I up the ante. "I think it'd be great to have her along."

I turn away, walk into the belly of the suite, drop my purse next to the couch and flop onto the cushion, my back to the new couple. I do not have to see Evie's face to know she's opening and closing her pretty little pink lips like a fish waiting for food.

"I … I … I think it'd be better for the three of you to meet alone for the first time. Especially since he's not even expecting you. He doesn't need an audience."

I smile to myself, think how easily I could make this even harder for Evie, but, she is my best friend, and, while I do not agree with her decision to keep Basil in the dark, I cannot betray her, nor can I stand seeing her so dang helpless.

"It'd be fine," Basil counters. "Evie doesn't count as an audience, does she?" he asks.

I turn to face them. Basil searches my face for agreement; Evie glowers. I contemplate making her squirm a little more, but when I open my mouth, she gives a pleading look and clasps her hands in front of her, prayerfully. I wink ever so quickly, get up, walk to the sliding glass door and look out at the city. "I think Evie is right."

I imagine her sigh mussing my hair from clear across the room.

)

Evie is ready and out the door within fifteen minutes. Fortunately, she left her Fitbit on the nightstand.

I grab for it, use it as an excuse. "She hates when she forgets this thing."

"I'll take it," Basil offers.

"You finish your orange. I'll try and catch her."

Evie has just stepped onto the elevator when I round the corner. I make a mad dash and slip in just before the doors close.

"What the—"

I hold out the Fitbit and wait for an explanation.

She fidgets with the watch, takes her time making sure she slips the fastener in an eye that won't leave the band too tight, then dangles her arms at her sides.

"Well?"

Evie's shoulders sag. The doors open and she steps forward. She wants out of the belly of the whale.

"Evie?"

She takes my wrist, pulls me out as others step on. "I don't want him to know, okay? I love him. I've never felt this way before. Not even with the ex. While you were gone we—"

I hold up a hand. "He's my brother. I don't want to know."

Evie blushes. "We mainly talked. Please, Violet. Let me do this my way."

I wrap Evie in a hug. "Don't hurt him. Please," I whisper.

"I won't. I promise," she breathes.

"And don't let him hurt you either," I say, leaning back, grasping her shoulders with my hands.

"Scouts honor," she says.

I smile, press the button, and step back into the elevator.

"You were never a girl scout," I say as the doors close, leaving Evie to do anything but shop while I pretend everything is okay.

☽

The elevator stops on the second floor. I nod a hello to the lady who joins me, noting that she is dressed completely in lavender (even her socks and shoes), but that's as far as my effort goes. I'm totally distracted by the conversation running through my mind, the one Evie and I had not too long ago, the one where she told me the news.

"Remember the guy I mentioned? The one I've been sorta seeing?"

"Yeah? You finally gonna tell me about him?" I'd asked, raising a brow as I pulled a towel out of the dryer and folded it first lengthwise then three flips down and stacked it on the one in the basket, flush edges out. "Do I know him?"

Evie was leaning against the washer, arms crossed. She knew better than to help me; she folds her socks in half, I tuck mine at the cuffs. I could only imagine how she might fold her towels.

"No. You don't know this guy."

"Will I get to meet him before we leave for New York?"

"That's what I want to talk to you about."

I halved a washcloth, then quartered it. I had a hunch. "You want him to come with us?"

"No. That wouldn't work."

"Why not?" Half, quarter, stack. Three to go.

"Because." Evie took a breath, closed her eyes and blurted, "He lives in New York."

I stifled the snap of a sheet. "Oh yeah? How'd you meet? Is he another one of those masseuse seminar gurus?" Evie had dated one before. He was okay until he asked if she'd like to clip his toenails and paint them for him before he took her on a surprise date. Evie never found out where he'd been planning to take her. She got a headache really fast and told him her clippers were dull.

"No. He's uhm … well …." Her eyebrows flattened. She all but squeezed her eyes shut.

"Oh. Come on. It can't be that bad," I'd said, as I folded a sheet in half. "Bad would be signing up on one of those online dating sites and chatting a guy up through cyberspace."

I laughed. Evie did not.

"Evie?" I questioned in the same tone I would use if she'd just finished off the last of my favorite banana pudding I'd been saving for later.

"It's not what you think," she said in a rush, hurrying on before I could respond. "You know that online book club I'm in? Well, we were reading *A Dog's Purpose*, and I got into this discussion with this guy, Victor, and he's *so* sweet. He has this beautiful black lab. I know because it's his little picture. Anyway, I told him I didn't have any animals and he said I should and I said what if I don't get the right one for me. He said I'd know the right one when I saw it. Anyway, we hit it off, kept on talking, and, kinda fell for each other."

I dropped the fitted sheet into the basket, folded my arms, and tried very hard to not come off as a mother hen. "You don't know anything about him. He could be feeding you a bunch of lies."

"You sound like a mother hen," Evie said. "Listen, I messaged him to see if he still wants to meet. We've talked about it before. When you said you were going to Nosilla, New York, I felt like it was a sign. That's where he lives. Anyway, he said he'd love to meet for coffee."

"He didn't mention you meeting him at his house?"

"No. That's what I'm sayin, silly. He's a real gentleman. He said he wanted to keep it public so I'd feel safe. He's aware of the creepiness of our relationship." She paused. "He said I'll know him by his orange suspenders."

This surprised me. "Wait. You don't know what he looks like?"

Evie shook her head. "He doesn't know what I look like either. My book club pic is a sunset. We decided to keep it a surprise."

"So you expect me to believe that neither of you have Facebook stalked?"

"I haven't. I swear."

"How do you know he hasn't?"

"Because he promised he wouldn't."

I couldn't help it. I rolled my eyes.

"Kinda hard considering we didn't share our last names."

"This is ludicrous. You could be talking to a serial killer!"

Evie sucked in her bottom lip and chewed.

"Why take this route to find a man?"

"I don't know. It just happened." She picked up one of my lone socks, that doesn't have a mate. She turned it inside-out and right-side-in over and over. "It's fun getting to know someone's mind first. And his knowledge of me is based totally on who I am inside, not whether or not my boobs are perky."

We both looked at her boobs. "Mehh," we said and shrugged.

"I don't know about this," I told her.

"You're the one who says everything happens for a reason. I truly believe your trip to New York is a sign that I'm finally supposed to meet him."

This reminded me of another question that'd been milling around in the back of my mind while I was processing this news. "How long have you been talking to this guy?"

"Six months."

"Six months! You've kept this a secret from me, your best friend, for six months?"

I was met with silence. Evie concentrated hard on my sock until I snatched it from her.

"I think if you are going to meet him, it's best this way. You'll have me and Basil close by. Who knows? Maybe we can meet him."

"He's really sweet. He's a—"

The front door creaked and Basil hollered, "Hello? Anyone home?"

"Do me a favor?" Evie requested. "Don't tell anyone. It's, well, it's kind of a weird situation."

"You're tellin me," I'd said, then drew her in for a hug. "Just be careful."

"In here," I called, then picked up the sheet, and returned to the task at hand.

☽

I return to the hotel room and find Basil painting a bouquet of flowers with his orange peel.

"Did you catch her?" he asks.

"Yep."

He dabs at the small canvas. "Are you okay with Evie and I being together?"

I rub my temples. "I just don't want either of you to get hurt."

"You'd be in the middle if it doesn't work out. That what you're afraid of?" He dabs here and there, shading a few of the petals.

"There's that. But you two are more important than *my* role in this. How's it going to work when you have to leave town? What if she is too clingy for your taste? How will holidays work if you two break up?" I stop, realizing what I've said. "Basil, I am so sorry. I am assuming a whole lot right now. You already have a family to spend holidays with."

He nods. "Yes. I have a family. One that's recently gotten bigger."

"This could get messy," I say thinking of his parents who still don't know about all this and a brother we have yet to meet.

"Isn't that what life's all about? The messy excitement that allows us to feel?" Basil asks, throwing the peel in the trash and appraising his work. He grabs a pen, signs the piece *Love, Basil,* leaves it on Evie's suitcase, then makes direct eye contact with me. "Let's do this."

"Waitin on you."

)

231 Enal is a tall, skinny dark brick building. We check the black mailboxes lining the cinderblock wall that juts out from the left of the building, obviously placed there to muffle the noise coming from the bakery on the ground floor next door. It did not, however, keep the delicious smell from wafting over.

"Our brother may very well be 300 pounds. I know I would be if I lived next door to a place that smells that much like heaven."

"Me too." I run my finger underneath the nameplate attached to each mailbox. T. Wilson is the last one. "He is in apartment …." I falter. Rather than numbers, these apartments have names. "Eliot. Bronte. Hardy. Homer. Tolstoy," I murmur. "Authors."

"Ha. That's pretty cool."

"Looks like Trip lives in apartment Tolstoy."

"Let's get after it."

We climb a bazillion winding stairs, bypassing four small square entryways.

"I take back what I said earlier," Basil huffs. "He can eat all the pastries he wants and still remain thin."

The hardwood creaks loudly beneath me. My heart starts pounding. What if Trip heard and we've been found out before we've even knocked? I breathe a sigh of relief when I hear no footsteps and the door remains closed. We are finally here, yet I am uncertain as to whether or not I'm ready to receive his reaction. I look at

Basil and whisper, "Our brother is on the other side of that door." Then I think to myself, *maybe he's singing while he makes lunch, or taking a nap with his cat, or watching a movie with his wife. Does he have a wife? Or a cat, for that matter?*

I follow Basil's gaze and join him in staring at the door as if it will produce answers.

Finally, Basil lifts the knocker. My pulse beats in time with the three heavy raps.

When no one answers, I bravely give the knocker a try. Still nothing.

"He must not be home."

Deflated, yet a little relieved, we trudge down the steps in silence. A surge of excitement courses through me when we pass a man on the stairs, but he lets himself into apartment Bronte.

☽

We are devouring macaroni and barbecue stuffed doughnuts next door to the apartment when my phone rings. It is mom. She is calling for an update and sounds a tad disappointed that we have no news. I never thought of it before, but I suppose, as a mother, she has to be over the moon excited at the possibility of being reunited with *all* of her children, though, when I'd asked if she'd like to join us, she'd refused.

"I gave my word I'd stay away, and that's what I'll do." She'd grinned. "You, on the other hand, did not make that promise."

I realize now that Mom has a lot riding on this visit.

"I'll let you know as soon as I know something."

We exchange our ritual *Goodbye, God bless, I love you's*, and end the call.

"How long do we wait?" I ask Basil.

"What? Oh." He looks up from his own phone. "Evie," he says, grinning, waving the phone.

"Is everything okay?" I'm suddenly worried. She hasn't texted me once, and I've been so wrapped up in finding Trip, I've barely thought of her. Guilt washes over me.

"Why wouldn't it be? She's shopping."

"Oh. Right," I say and take the last bite of my doughnut. "Did she say how much longer she's going to be?" I ask and point to the appetizer. "Are you going to eat that fried pickle?"

"Let's split it," he says, picking up the golden crusted pickle and putting it on his plate to cut. "And, yes, she said she was ready to head back to the hotel, but when I told her our dilemma, she said she'd find another shop or two to keep her occupied until we're finished." He hands me my half. "She says the room would be boring without me."

I feign a hurt expression.

"But I'm sure she meant us," he says, a wry smile on his face as he gestures his pickle between himself and me. "I told her I'd text when we are finished."

"I'll just bet she meant *us*," I tease, then think out loud, "I wonder why she didn't text *me*."

"You aren't as good a kisser," Basil says with an eyebrow cocked as he takes a drink of his water.

I wad up the napkin in my hand and throw it at him. It is then that my phone chimes. "Ha ha. There she is now, I'll bet."

But when I check the text, I find a single heart staring back at me. Grayson.

☽

Lunch, start to finish, takes less than thirty minutes.

"Should we try back?" I ask.

"Let's give it a little longer." Basil is not looking at me. I follow his gaze and see a man kneeling before a stunning blond. He offers her a ring. When she nods, I applaud, as do others who have noticed the proposal.

The man slips the ring on her finger, stands, folds the woman in his arms and kisses her. Then he ushers her into the café.

I return my attention to Basil, who is madly sketching in an art book he brought along in his backpack. His hand is a flurry of motion. I watch, mesmerized, as he recreates the proposal. In the twenty minutes it takes him to capture the moment, I realize I've been sitting motionless, as if he's drawing me. He scribbles his name and the date in a section of the sidewalk he's recreated, then reaches in his pack and retrieves a sticker that he affixes to the back. He finishes off his drink, then glances again at the couple.

"You gonna give it to them?" I ask.

Basil shrugs. "I think so."

The man slides his chair back and disappears into the restaurant.

"You'll have to wait until he comes back now," I say, watching the restaurant door close behind him.

Basil looks back at the table, sees that the man is gone, and leaps to his feet. "Be right back," he says, and makes his way across the patio.

He gives the woman the drawing, and, though I don't hear what's being said, I can see the look of joy on her face as she stands to give him a hug.

He all but runs back to our table, picks up his backpack and says, "Let's get outta here."

I follow him down the street, hurrying to keep up. "The apartment's back there."

"I know. We'll just go around the block. Burn some time."

"Okay," I say, uncertain as to why Basil is acting a little like Jason Bourne. "That was really sweet. What you did back there."

When we turn the corner, he slows down. "I don't usually make personal deliveries, and I really didn't want any additional thanks from the guy, hence the quick take off."

"So you do this often?"

Basil shrugs. "Often enough."

"Why?"

"Coupla reasons. When I see something as pure and wonderful as that, I have to capture it. I try to leave it without being noticed. I'm kinda shy like that."

He bats his lashes to make light of the truth he's revealed.

I chuckle.

"Sometimes, I have no choice. Like today. I wanted them to have the drawing. At least the guy went back inside. So, it was sorta undercover." He shrugs. "It's nice to make people happy. But I don't like a lot of hoopla to go with it. I don't do it for the ooh's and ahh's. That makes me uncomfortable."

"You're gonna have a heck of a time when you become a famous artist."

Basil forces a laugh. "When I leave them for people to discover, it's fun to watch from a distance. They look around trying to figure out if the person who left it might still be around, then they contemplate whether or not it's okay to take it."

"You little devil."

"It's a riot. What can I say?"

We've made our way back to Trip's apartment building.

"Think he's up there?"

"Don't know." Basil readjusts his backpack. "Let's go see."

On our way up the bazillion steps, I ask Basil, "So what's the other reason, you give your art away?"

He glances over his shoulder at me. "No one'll know who you are if they never see your art."

"Hmm."

"It's a form of marketing for me. I put my information on the back."

"What will you do when you are discovered? You'll have to talk to people about your work then."

"I'll cross that bridge when I get to it," he says, rounding the banister. "Artists are a funny breed. Lots of us are introverts who want our work to be known without having to put *ourselves* on display. Which makes the whole discovery process a tricky business."

"You know why I think you do it?"

He looks at me, confused. "Do what?"

"Give people gifts like that."

"Why's that?"

He steps onto the fifth floor square of hallway, Tolstoy, and waits for me.

"Because you are a good person," I say, looping my arm around his.

We are standing in front of Trip's door.

"Ready?" Basil asks, arching his brow.

"As I'll ever be."

))

A mass of long auburn curls answers the door. For a moment, I believe we've intruded on Cousin It. But when the owner of said curls pulls them back into a messy man bun, I see my mother's eyes and the shape of her chin.

"Can I help you?" he asks, looking at me, then Basil, then back at me again.

My phone is buzzing, telling me there's a text. Immediately, I think of Evie, but I'm stuck in this moment.

"What's a matter? Cat got your tongue?" He angles his head, and cocks a brow just as Basil did, not two minutes ago. I can't help but stare.

"We are here to see Trip Wilson," Basil manages as he too gawks openly.

The man zeroes in on Basil; I take the opportunity to check my text. Not Evie. Grayson again. But I don't have time to read it. Not now. I drop my phone back into the mouth of my purse.

"You look awfully familiar," the man says to Basil.

"Are you Trip Wilson?"

"What if I am?"

"Uhm, well, then ...."

"Look, I paid all my parking tickets and sold the bloody car. You're not getting another dime out of me." He steps back to close the door. I stop it with my hand.

"Lady, you need to get off my property."

"We aren't here about tickets."

He looks at me. Hard. "*You* look familiar, too," he says, squinting. "Did I date you?" He shakes his head. "Look, no way it's my kid."

I am taken aback. Both my brothers have thought of me sexually. I kind of gag. Basil laughs, breaking the tension.

"You've got it all wrong," he says.

"Well, I don't want what you're selling, I'm not hiring, and I pray on my own, so I don't need your help." He stops. "Although, it would be kinda nice to have someone to pray with. I've always wondered if Mormons pray differently than Christians."

"We aren't Mormon," I say.

"Ahh, Jehovah's Witness, then."

"Huh-uh," Basil says.

"Well then." The man scratches the scruff on his chin. "Look, I'm sort of in the middle of something, so if you'll excuse me." He moves to close the door again.

"We are family," I blurt out.

His brows knot. "Family?"

"Yes. The three of us," I say, circling my finger in the space between us.

"How?"

I want very much to say something smart alecky like, *Your dad and my mom loved each other so much they created three babies at once,* but I refrain.

"Trip?" I ask, making certain he is who I know he is.

He nods.

"May we come in?"

I don't know if I'd have been as welcoming, but he releases the door and steps aside.

☽

Trip's apartment is beautiful. The front wall facing the street is brick; the others pine. Plenty of windows keep the place from being too dark. The entire space is open, but, based on furniture placement, it is fairly easy to delineate what serves as living room, dining room, and studio. The place is full of all sorts of potted plants and herbs, some I can name, others I cannot.

Trip paces from his baby grand piano to a small bar situated on the far wall. His bare feet make a sticking sound on the hardwood floor as he traipses back and forth.

We remain in the dining room just inside the door and Basil does the talking. He does not stop moving until Basil finishes with, "And that's all we know."

"So, you expect me to believe that I am adopted and that my father, Richard Wilson, did not fertilize my mother's egg, and that my precious mother, Anne Wilson, did not give birth to me?"

Basil looks at me quizzically, as if to say, *Is this guy for real?* I have to admit, Trip has a strange way with words. I picture Basil circling a finger at his temple and have to fake a cough to keep from laughing.

"That about sums it up," I answer.

"And the two of you met by falling for each other?"

"Yep." I fidget with a green glass coaster that sits on a black marble stand beside me. Somehow I found it among the plants that fountain over it.

"And, my mother wants to meet me? Yet she gave me and you away?" He points to Basil. "But not you?" He points at me.

"Yep," I say again.

"And she wants to meet me?" he repeats.

"Yep."

"But she threw me away."

I stand a little taller, forget the coaster, and close the space between myself and Trip. Before I can defend my mother, Basil chimes in. "It wasn't like that. Did you not hear anything I said?"

Trip flops into a chair that hangs from a beam in the living room ceiling, drops his head in his hands, and massages his temples.

Without invitation, Basil and I situate ourselves on the loveseat next to him. "Listen," I say, "I know this is a lot of information. Believe me, when I found out, I freaked."

"I reckon so. You almost did the hanky-panky with your own—"

"Enough," I say, waving a hand in the air.

"We didn't get nearly that far," Basil adds.

"Thank God for small miracles. At least your mother had enough sense to keep that train from entering the tunnel. I swear, I don't understand people who don't take care of their responsibilities."

"You know what?" I say, having had enough. "It is clear you haven't listened at all. Mom was alone. She had no money. She wanted what was best for us." I open my arms wide. "You've apparently done well for yourself. It sounds like you adore your parents, and yet, you are full of sass concerning my ... our mother.

"I know this is a shock, and I'm sure you need time to process, but we are your brother and sister and we wanted very much to meet you. But, if you don't want to know us, then, well ... c-ya." I stand and make my way to the door. Basil follows.

My hand is on the knob when Trip says, "Can I see a picture of her? Our mother?"

I let out a breath I didn't know I'd been holding. "Sure," I say, the sharp edge gone from my tone.

I scroll through my photos, trying to find the very best one. I recall a picture I took last summer of Mom standing in her garden when it was in full bloom. Her hair was frizzing all over; her eyes full of joy. She was the most beautiful flower in the midst of all the glorious bursts of color. I want Trip to see how lovely she is; I want him to see how much they look alike.

As I search, Trip apologizes. "It's a lot to take in. All this time I thought I had a biological mom and dad, and one brother by the same parents, and now, I feel like I've been living a lie. I have four parents and I share a birthday with two additional siblings I didn't know existed."

"It threw us too, man," Basil confesses.

"Sure did," I admit as I continue to scroll through my camera roll. "Here it is," I say, clicking the screen to enlarge the picture, but before I can share it with him, there's a quick knock at the door followed by, perhaps, the oddest hello I've ever heard.

"We are the music makers, and we are the dreamers of the dreams," says a tall, silver-haired beauty as he lets himself in.

Trip navigates around his plants, putting himself between us and the striking gentleman. "My father likes to speak in quotes," Trip says by way of introduction. "Willy Wonka and the Chocolate Factory. 1971." Then, without warning, he adds, "Dad, this is Basil and Violet, my brother and sister."

Mr. Wilson extends a hand, begins with, "Very nice to mee—" before stopping short. He steps back and peers at us. "You're what? Have you joined a church?"

I stifle a laugh, thinking, *As if he can't see the resemblance*, but then who am I to judge? I hadn't recognized the similarities between myself and Basil. I blame the beard for that.

Basil does not hide his amusement. Trip, however, does not so much as hint at a smile. "Why didn't you tell me?"

"Tell you what?"

"Are you serious? You are going to pretend you had no idea when the proof is right before you?"

Mr. Wilson looks totally confused.

Trip rolls his eyes. "Basil. Violet. Would you mind giving us some time?"

I shrug. "Yeah. Sure. But, well, we'll be leaving in a couple of days."

"Leave your number." Trip makes his way to the kitchen, rummages through what appears to be a junk drawer, and fishes out a pen and paper on which I write my number and Basil's. I leave both pen and message on a counter made of pennies. *What a beautiful piece,* I think. *Too bad the beauty of it is almost completely covered with plants.*

"I'll be in touch soon," he says.

Trip opens the door and ushers us out. "Today. I'll be in touch today," he promises, leaving us in the hall, a goodbye stuck in my throat like a noodle that slipped down prematurely and is trying to reemerge.

I am not gonna lie. I really want to stay and eavesdrop, which is why I am relieved when I see Basil lean in. Fortunately for us, the door is thin and Trip makes no effort to invite his father further into the jungle.

"Am I adopted?"

"Well, what … what do you mean adopted?"

"You aren't a stupid man. Come on, Dad. Am I adopted?"

"Well now, son. It's not that simple."

"Oh, but it is. See, the two people you just met are claiming to be my brother and sister."

"Could be after your money. Or mine."

I imagine Trip's eyes making another round. "Oh for the love of God. Are you serious? People don't research *man with successful plant business with father who does well in real estate* and decide to come swindle us."

"Well son, see, well...."

I whisper to Basil. "If that guy says *well* one more time—"

Basil puts a finger to his lips.

"They look just like me, Dad. And they're the same age. We share the same sad day-after-Christmas birthday, for heaven's sake."

"Why would *they* not have been adopted? Tell me that. How come you were the only one given up?"

"I wasn't. And you know it. Don't you? And Mom. But she never said anything either."

There is a long pause. I imagine a stand-off. Two men staring each other down, waiting to see what the other will do.

"Tell me the truth."

"The truth?"

"You've never lied to me before. Or at least I thought you hadn't."

"All I wanted to do was shelter you. Bring you up as normal as possible."

"Being adopted makes me abnormal?"

"Being adopted into a family that splits up certainly isn't what I'd hoped for you. There was a lot going on. I didn't think it was necessary to add anything else."

"Does Pickle know?"

I assume Mr. Wilson shakes his head because Trip follows with, "I guess if you didn't tell me, you wouldn't tell my brother."

Another very long silence followed by, "Why did you adopt me?"

"Because your mother and I couldn't have children."

"But you did. I mean, I've heard of that happening before. Couples adopt and then the miracle baby is conceived. Were you sorry you adopted me after, you know, you and mom got pregnant with Pickle?"

I mouth the name *Pickle* to Basil. He shrugs.

"Of course not."

There's some shuffling around the door. I worry Trip will open it and find us. I hold my breath and do not move. My feet are cemented to the floor. Luckily, the conversation resumes and we aren't caught.

"It's not what you think," Mr. Wilson says.

"Why don't you explain then, *Dad*?" The emphasis on Dad makes both Basil and I wince.

"Pickle doesn't know what I'm about to tell you."

"Ooh, the plot thickens," Trip says.

"I can't have children. Apparently, your mother can."

It takes a moment for Trip to catch on. "Wait a minute. You can't be serious? My mother? My precious Anne?"

"Cheated on me with another man," Mr. Wilson says. "Pickle isn't my biological son. He's Will's son."

"Does Will know?"

"Of course he does."

"Does Pickle know you aren't his father?"

"I just told you Pickle knows nothing about what I'm telling you."

"How the heck does that work? Will raises Pickle as a step-father? But he's actually his biological father? Come to think of it, Pickle does have the same nose as Will. How could you keep this from me?"

"We thought it best that the two of you never know."

"That's bull!"

I'll say, I whisper.

"I'm telling him."

"Son, look. When we found out your mom was pregnant, you were three. My heart was broken. I wanted to have some sense of normal. I wanted you to feel safe and secure. You are my world."

"But Pickle doesn't know Will is his father! You sacrificed his feelings for mine. All three of you did! That's not right."

"Will and your mother felt guilty and I took advantage of that."

"Don't defend them."

"I was angry and just wanted the heck out of there."

"So you took me and left. I always wondered why Pickle got to stay with Mom. Didn't she want me?"

"Of course she did. But, and I'm ashamed to say this, I used you Trip. I'd lost everything. I didn't want to lose you, too. I told them I'd leave and not make any waves as long as I got to take you with me."

Silence.

"I can't believe this …. So that's why Pickle rarely came here. All this time, he's thought his own father didn't want him. He's told me that. That he thinks of Will as his father because Will had time for him and you never did. He's always thought I'm your favorite and Mom's favorite because of how she made an effort to see me. You never tried to see him."

"Now you know why."

"He should've been told."

"I wanted to protect you."

"At his expense?"

"Your mother wanted to tell him. But Will, he was once my best friend. He talked her out of it on more than one occasion. The guilt of loving his best friend's girl has always plagued him …. Guess we should probably have a talk with Pickle, huh?"

"Ya think?"

"I'll call Anne."

"Did you know I had a brother and sister?"

Mr. Wilson must nod. "But I didn't know any details."

"Gee gads, Dad. What now?"

"Cat's outta the bag. May as well get to know your brother and sister."

"I think I will."

"Remember one thing, Trip."

"What's that?"

"I'm your number one fan."

"Misery. 1990," Trip replies, then opens the door, and we stumble in.

☽

"You guys would make terrible private investigators. You didn't even try to make it sound like you were leaving. Some fake footsteps would've been nice."

"Are you mad?"

"Truthfully, I have no idea what I am. I have never lived a day such as this one. I am likely in shock. Definitely in need of some herb, but I'll refrain for now. Only because I want to take you to dinner. Get to know you."

Mr. Wilson, who is standing at the kitchen counter, drinking RC straight out of a two-liter bottle, unseals his lips, lets out a small belch, and walks toward us. "Forgive me for any harm that's come your way because of my own selfishness."

"For what it's worth, my parents didn't tell me either. Heck, they still don't know I know," Basil admits.

"Yeah. The only reason we know is because we started dating."

"My word!" Mr. Wilson says as if he's straight from the South.

"We used to live in Georgia," Trip explains without my having to ask. "Anne still lives there."

"We use that phrase in Virginia, too."

After that, no one knows what to say. One thing's for sure, we've had our fill of awkward silences for the day.

"How about dinner tonight? Say six? There's this lovely restaurant right here in Nosilla."

"We are staying not far from here."

"Absolute slice of heaven, this place."

I wonder if he's been to Secretsville. It too is heavenly. I think of the unopened text and my heart skips a beat.

"Anyway. Eel Street Restaurant for dinner, and there's a lovely ice cream shop just a little ways down Enal. We can go there after. Sound good?"

"Sounds great," Basil agrees.

"May we bring our friend?" I ask.

"Absolutely," Mr. Wilson says.

"I'll bring my girlfriend," Trip says.

"Sounds good," Basil and I say at the same time.

I check my watch. It's nearing 4:30. Just enough time to freshen up. "Guess we'll see you soon then," I say.

Mr. Wilson opens the door for us. We are barely down the stairs when he says to Trip, "I'm sorry I was such a saint before, and I'm such a prick now."

I'm guessing this is his way of saying he's sorry if Trip's view of him has changed now that the secret is out.

Though I am not part of the exchange, I can't help looking back to reply, "Family Man. 2000."

Mr. Wilson winks and closes the door.

☽

I check Grayson's text as we wait to cross the street.

I miss you.

I ask myself if I miss him too and realize I've had too much going on in the past several hours to give Grayson much thought. But when I do think of him, I feel a warmth inside like no other. It's that feel good sensation that comes when you take a deep breath after a summer rain. Or when you get the perfect mix of hot fudge and vanilla ice cream in a bite of sundae. I decide to keep it simple—I send a smiley face. On the heels of warm fuzzy come the reality that a relationship with Grayson will never work. Our roots run too deep.

Basil and I somehow get turned around and have to pick up the pace to get back to the hotel and get ready.

Evie is waiting for us.

"So, how did it go?"

"How was shopping?" I ask at the same time.

"Okay," we both reply.

"You first," she says. Clearly we cannot talk about where she really was.

"We're going to dinner and you're invited." Basil crosses the room and kisses Evie on the cheek.

I check my watch. "Dinner is in less than an hour," I say heading for my suitcase.

As we freshen up and change, we fill Evie in as best we can in such a short time.

"Trip is sassy," I say.

"I felt so bad for his dad," Basil offers, spitting toothpaste in the sink.

"Overall it went well, though?"

"It's a lot to take in. I felt kinda bad for them."

"You went through the same thing," Evie reminds me, then asks, "Do you guys look alike?"

"I guess. We all have freckles. Our eyes are different colors. Did you notice that Basil?"

"No. What's that?" Basil is distracted by the iron he cannot seem to turn on.

Evie flips a switch on the side. "I ironed a few things earlier," she says. "Just in case we decided to go out."

"Anyway," I continue, "my eyes are brown. Basil's are green, and Trip's are blue."

"That's weird."

"I thought so too."

"His dad is handsome."

"Yeah?"

"A little George Clooney-ish."

"Nah. I don't think so," Basil disagrees, then changes his mind. "Maybe a little. It's the hair I think. Maybe a little around the eyes, too."

"How did *he* react?" Evie asks.

"Mehh. Out of sorts. Not sure what to say. It was messy. We eavesdropped at the door and got caught."

I fill Evie in on that embarrassment as we grab our key card and depart. She gets a charge out of this, and, for a moment, the nervous tension I noticed in her earlier, vanishes.

I am struck by just how beautiful my best friend is. She's wearing a pair of white capris with a navy top and gold sandals. Her blonde hair is blowing lightly in a breeze that, by the way, hints of a near-by hotdog stand. And her face simply glows when she is anywhere near Basil, yet this evening there's a hint of anxiety about her.

Basil is wearing khakis and white shirt, fashionably untucked. He's handsome, strutting along in his sandals, backpack over his shoulder, holding Evie's hand. I take in the sight of them and see a perfect couple. This makes me happy.

I tell myself the apprehension I sense in Evie is normal for someone still processing a break-up. She's been talking to Victor for months. Even though she'd never technically met the guy, they'd had an emotional connection. It couldn't have been easy to end things the first time they saw each other in person. I can't wait to get the details on how everything went.

My thoughts return to the evening ahead. I am excited to see my brother again, get the chance to talk with him, ask him questions the roller coaster of emotions did not stop for earlier. So much has happened in such a short time.

We stop at the crosswalk and wait for the signal. Evie takes my hand and gives it a squeeze. "I'm looking forward to meeting—" she begins but is interrupted by two rather substantial women who spill out of a pizza joint in a flurry of flailing arms and cursing. They smack at each other as they hurl insults back and forth. We are all three caught off guard by the disruption and cannot help gawking.

All I can gather from the yelling is that one spent the rent money on a pair of boots and a down payment on a boob job.

"Ain't no doctor gonna make 'em bigger for under a thousand. You ain't got no sense."

"Das what he said. Dis girl wit im said he did hers."

"Das bull and you know it. Dey's scammin you. Now, how we gonna get by? Guess ol slum doc do up ya boobs and I'll sit under em when it rains. Closest thing a shelter I's gonna get."

Evie cracks up.

The larger of the two women whirls on her. "Whatchoo over der snickerin bout?"

Evie sobers. "No-nothing," she swears.

"Das right. Nothin."

Her friend takes the opportunity to try and get away.

"Fool," the woman calls, taking two giant steps and snatchin the woman by the hair.

Fool screams like a cat.

Now, one would think that, since one of us had just been called out, we'd take the opportunity the good Lord gave us and leave. But, we don't. Despite the fact that we are likely going to be late, that we are no match for these women who look like they could take on a dozen marines and win, we continue watching this train derail.

"Get offa me, Gertie." Fool starts wailing on her with fists that won't quite close due to the daggers for fingernails she has.

Gertie's eyes get so big the brown irises look small in comparison to the whites. They remind me of fried eggs, somehow. She places her hand on Fool's forehead and stretches her arm so the blows just barely graze her. Then, she takes her purse, a long wide thing, and begins beating Fool in the head, yelling, "Take dem boots back. It's goin on summa. You don't need em. And you better find dat Mista Ignorant and get dat money back for dem boobs you ain't gettin.'" She says this in rhythm with the thumping of her purse.

"Ladies!" I hear Evie shout, and that's when I know she's snapped into corrections officer mode. "Enough!" she says, stepping behind Gertie, pulling her arm behind her back. This gives Fool just enough time to remove a drink from a passersby and fling it all over Gertie, and, inevitably Evie's white pants.

☽

Evie orders the ladies out of the middle of the sidewalk. Unfortunately, they are too far away for us to hear more than bits and pieces of the conversation.

Basil wears a concerned expression, his posture tense, ready to intervene if necessary. But it isn't. Evie manages to befriend these women in minutes and make them care about what she thinks of them.

In the end, both Gertie and Fool (that's truly the name she answers to) hug Evie and thank her. Basil is completely in awe at this point.

"How did you do that?" he asks as Evie rejoins us. "How did you diffuse that complete mess?"

"It's all in how you talk to them. What's going on in their world is important, and you have to let them know you understand that. I helped them determine a game plan for getting back the boob job money, and I told Fool the truth about the boots—if she doesn't have the money, it doesn't matter how good a sale it is, she needs to return them. A roof over her head is more important. Her lip drooped so low, I thought she might trip on it, but, she agreed to take them back."

"My goodness, I love you," Basil says and plants a kiss on her lips. He looks at her clothes. "You're a mess."

"Yeah."

"Think they'll get their money back?" I ask.

"Heavens no," Evie says. "But, they'll team up trying to search that guy out. The adventure of it will keep their friendship safe."

"And the money you slipped in her purse will cover the loss," Basil says to me.

"You weren't supposed to see that."

☽

We enter the restaurant seven minutes late.

"I'm gonna help Evie get cleaned up," I tell Basil. "You'll explain, won't you?"

"Sure" he says, making his way to the hostess who, when I approach just behind Basil and ask, "Bathroom?" points behind us and to the left.

We leave Basil asking after the Wilson party.

As soon as we've closeted ourselves in the bathroom, I pounce. "Why didn't you text me after you saw Victor?"

Evie grabs several cloths from a stack, gets them wet, adds a little hand soap and dabs at the stains. "I didn't want to take the chance of Basil accidentally seeing something he shouldn't, and I wasn't up for covert code" she says, focusing on her pants.

"How did the break-up go?"

Evie's shoulders slump and she looks up. She doesn't have to say a word.

"You didn't do it," I state.

"It's complicated."

"Complicated?" I gasp. "Complicated?" I point toward the restaurant. "You want complicated, try having dinner with two brothers that, not even a month ago, you didn't know you had. And now, here we are: My best friend is dating one of my brothers, and she hasn't broken up with her Internet boyfriend yet," I hiss as softly as possible because there's someone in one of the stalls and the bathroom attendant isn't all that far away.

"Your life isn't the only one turned upside-down."

I take a deep breath. "Evie, I know that. And I'm sorry to act like I've got more to handle than you do. I shouldn't have reacted like that. But, well, I really don't want to see you start a relationship this way. I want you and Basil to be able to trust each other."

"And I want to keep him. I love him. I don't want to drive him away. And this … this mess I'm in could do that."

"Why didn't you break it off with Victor?"

"Because." She hesitates.

"What?" I ask, grabbing another cloth and getting it wet.

"Victor was married."

"While you guys were talking?" I shriek.

"Shh," Evie says, looking at the attendant who discretely looks away. "No. He's been divorced for a little over a year."

"So, you were a rebound."

"Gee thanks."

The toilet flushes and we wait as an employee washes her hands to the tune of Happy Birthday before sending a questioning glance the attendant's way as if to say, *Keep an eye on these crazies*, and leaves.

"His wife of ten years did something terrible. She broke his trust. I feel bad for him. I just couldn't dump him the very first time we met."

"What did she do? His wife?"

We exchange cloths. I rinse the dirty ones and reach for another. The attendant clears her throat. "Last one," I promise.

"Victor wanted kids. His wife didn't. She went behind his back and had her tubes tied."

"Oh my word."

"Yep." Evie continues dabbing. "I don't want to make him think all women are terrible. He's super nice."

"What do you plan to do?"

"Text him on our way back to Virginia."

For a moment, all I can do is stand before my best friend and gape. Finally, I manage, "How is that better than breaking it off in person?"

"I don't know. It just is. It's less real that way."

"Sorta like the *relationship* you've been carrying on with him?"

Evie throws the soiled cloth on the counter. "Look. I love Basil. And I want to be with him. What Victor and I had was special, but it's over."

"Have. You haven't ended it," I correct.

"In my head and heart it's over."

"Breaking up with him over text is hideous, you know? You're going to have to see him again."

"He wants to, I think. I told him I'm leaving tonight."

"You lied to him?"

"I don't want to see him again. I just want out of this mess."

"Do you think texting him it's over is going to make him trust women any more than if you'd been honest with him?"

Evie places a foot on the wall and turns her leg awkwardly so her soaked quad is under the dryer while the rest of her body is turned toward me. She jabs the button with her elbow. "I didn't say I'd really thought anything through," she says, competing with the sound of the dryer. "I more or less reacted. Exactly the opposite of what I'm trained to do."

"Well, you're awesome at your job, but you've got some work to do in the personal life area."

Evie looks at me, clearly peeved. "Talked to Grayson?" she asks, giving me a quick smart alecky grin.

"Touché," I offer, checking my watch. "We've gotta get out here."

"I'm a mess," she says turning the dryer on again.

"I'm sure Basil has already explained."

I place a hand on Evie's shoulder and say, "Love you no matter what."

"Right back at ya." She drops her foot to the floor. "This'll have to do," she says of the damp beige stain on her pants.

"Let's go see my other long lost bro."

We pass the attendant who immediately moves to clean up our pile of cloths. "He brought his girlfriend, you know? And his dad."

"A good ol family reunion," Evie says.

"Yeah right. That."

☽

The hostess leads us through the restaurant to our table. Piano music floats lightly through the air like a stream of butterflies, soft and beautiful. The place sparkles with strands of white lights crisscrossing the ceiling, planters, posts, and beams. Even the volcano lamp centerpieces are stuffed with tiny white lights.

Something catches Evie's eye. She points. "Is that?" she begins and walks toward a familiar 11X14 of the bridge and creek at Dickey Ridge, positioned in the second of five windowsills along the wall.

I follow, explaining what Basil told me earlier about gaining exposure.

"Pardon me," Evie says to the people sitting at the table by the window. She picks it up, runs a hand over it lovingly. "I know this man," she tells the couple.

"Really?" the woman asks, intrigued.

This begins an in-depth conversation about how wonderful and talented Basil is.

I hear a huff behind me and turn to see a rather irritated hostess.

"Oh," I say, smiling weakly. "Sorry."

I tap Evie on the shoulder, but she doesn't respond.

The hostess interrupts. "Your table is in the back on the far right. I have other guests to see to, so...," she says, trying to hurry us along without seeming rude.

Evie glances at the hostess's nametag. "Samantha, you've been so patient. I'm sorry to have kept you. I'll be a minute more. Y'all go on without me."

Samantha nods and addresses me. "Would you like me to show you to your table?"

"No, no. I'll find my way. Thank you. Sorry," I tell her and leave Evie midway through the recollection of the day Basil saw the very bear he's painted splashing through the creek.

I see Trip's long strawberry curls first and the profile of his face. I don't know that I'll ever get used to seeing this version of my mother. Basil is laughing heartily at something a woman, whose back is to me, is saying. Mr. Wilson, wine glass in hand, raises it when he sees me approaching.

"Perhaps it is good to have a beautiful mind, but an even greater gift is to have a beautiful heart." He stands, pulls out the chair beside him. "Forgive anything you may have overhead me saying earlier when you were eavesdropping. I was taken a bit off guard."

I smile, thank him for holding my chair, and reply, "That quote sounds like it would've been used in A Beautiful Mind, which came out in ..." I have to think a second, "2001?"

He nods his approval.

"But I don't recall that dialogue."

Trip turns to me. "It's from a deleted scene."

"How do you know that?" I ask.

"Try living with *him* your whole life," he says, nodding toward his father. "He's always played this little trivia game with me. A better question is, how come you're so good at it? That's twice in one day."

"Something I've always been interested in," I say, looking beyond Trip to the stunning beauty seated at his left. "Who's this?"

Trip slips his arm around a lovely woman with skin the color of caramel. She has a messy afro, ends dyed red, a firework raining down around a flawless face, "This is my lady, Kiwi."

Kiwi half stands, reaches across Trip, and extends a hand. "A pleasure to meet you, friend." She looks from me to Trip to Basil. "Amazing," she says. "A truly amazing gift, the three of you finding one another."

I am unable to take my eyes off Kiwi. Her voice is deep and rusty, a frog turned princess. Her lips are thick and painted a deep purple to match the lavender dress that shows off curves in all the right places.

"Everything okay?" she asks.

I blink. "Yes," I say. "It's just … you are simply stunning."

"As are you."

I can't help thinking the compliment has to be Kiwi's way of removing herself from the center of attention. Yet, she doesn't strike me as the type to offer insincere praise. Still, I do not see myself in the same league as her.

"Daisies and Petunias look very different but are equally beautiful," she says, reading my mind.

"I could listen to you speak all day."

"Are you flirting with my girlfriend?" Trip asks.

I feel my face get hot. "Maybe," I say.

Everyone around the table laughs.

I take a rather long drink of chardonnay.

"Where's Evie?" Basil asks.

"Talking to a couple about a painting she noticed." I don't give any further details. If Basil wants anyone to know his secret marketing strategy, it's his business to elaborate.

"Ahh," he says. "Hope she's soon on her way. I can't wait for you to meet her," he says to the others. "She's … I can't capture the words," he says.

"She's okay," I joke, filling the awkward space only new love can create.

He looks around searching her out, turns back to me and mouths a quick silent thank you. I wonder what he's grateful for, keeping his art display a secret or covering the wound cupid's clearly left.

I spot Evie weaving between tables and wave, getting her attention.

"Basil," she says, approaching. "You are a genius."

"Evie," I interrupt before she can out him, "this is our brother, Trip."

Evie turns, clearly realizing her misplaced attention in the given situation. Her reaction is not, however, the pleasant *nice to meet you* I expect.

Her jaw drops along with every ounce of color in her face. I turn to Trip apologetically but notice he is varying degrees of red. It seems no one else is in the room but the two of them.

The silence seems to stretch into eternity when in reality it's a split second, one in which, neither of the two is thinking clearly since, what follows is a truth I am certain they never intended to share.

"Evie?" Trip asks, song-like.

I am vaguely aware of Basil's head swiveling back and forth, back and forth searching Evie's shocked expression and then Trip's. Next comes a chorus of sorts from everyone present: "You know each other?" followed by Evie, who adds to the main lyric Trip started: "Victor?"

I am the needle scratching the record, ending this wretched song and dance. "No," I say, covering my mouth. "No way."

My best friend does a one-eighty and runs out.

Basil does not excuse himself, nor does he make an effort to right his chair that clatters to the floor as he goes after Evie.

Trip looks at Kiwi who's staring at him, her right brow curved in an amazing arch that reminds me of a gymnast doing a backflip, and says, "I can explain."

127

Mr. Wilson, obviously close enough to his son to be privy to the same details Evie has entrusted to me, puts two and two together at about the same speed I do, downs his wine, pours another, and says, "God's nightgown!"

I drain my own glass as I get to my feet. Uncertain of where I'm headed, but very aware that I have to get the heck out of the eye of this storm, I call over my shoulder while racing toward the exit, "Gone with the Wind. 1939."

☽

I intentionally go in the opposite direction of the hotel. One right turn and two lefts leaves me standing in Huckleberry Park. The trees are pruned so that they look like lollipops, while the bushes that line the loop of cobblestone path take a variety of shapes—a phone booth, a soldier, George Jetson. I wonder if Edward Scissorhands was here, until I read the information board that gives credit to Dandelion Troy's Garden Club. I make one full loop before checking my phone for a text. Nothing. Basil and Evie must really be having a humdinger of a fight. I can't help but selfishly wonder where this will leave me. Will it be difficult for Basil to visit now? Will he still want to visit? Will Evie steer clear when he's in town? Will my and Evie's friendship change? And, what about Trip? What will he say to Kiwi? Will this be the end for them? Will he ever agree to meet Mom?

Mom. I pull out my phone and call before I consider what she's going to want to talk about and exactly how much I'm willing to divulge at this point.

"Moonbeam," I hear after the second ring. I love that Dad calls me this. It always brings a sense of comfort.

"Hey, Dad," I say, my voice strained.

"Honey, are you okay?"

"Oh. Yeah." I pinch the bridge of my nose. "I was just thinking how much I adore hearing you call me Moonbeam."

"You are the light of my life," Dad says.

I walk by a bush trimmed to look like a man holding his naked privates.

"You know," Mom says, "I had your middle name narrowed down to either Moon or the place you were conceived."

I picture the two of them—Dad on the phone in the kitchen, Mom in the living room on the other, looking at Dad as she talks.

"I don't think I want to know," I say.

"Kmart."

"You went?" I ask thinking she's changed the subject. "Is there one close to Front Royal I don't know about?" The one in town recently closed.

"That would've been your middle name, but I went with Moon because it sounds so pretty with my last name—Beam."

It suddenly becomes clear. Dad's nickname for me is my very first given name. This thought swims to the back of my mind as another takes its place on the surface. My mother has just admitted where she'd had her one night stand, and I am a wee bit appalled.

"Kmart?" I ask, stopping in front of another bush, a large green crayon that actually has the word *forest green* engraved neatly up the side.

"In the men's big-and-tall section. I thought I told you that."

I continue walking. "Nope. No ya didn't. I think I'm sorry you told me now." *The Kmart big-and-tall department*, I think to myself, and all at once, I am laughing hysterically, then I'm crying.

"Everything okay?" Dad asks.

I sniff and wipe my eyes, avoiding the stares of three homeless men and their scruffy dog. "Yeah. Sure. Everything's good. Just a long day. And, I can't believe my name could have been Violet Kmart Beam."

"Violet?" Mom says, having delayed long enough. I know my mother. She's been attempting to refrain from bombarding me, and now, she's about to burst. I know exactly what she is going to ask.

"Yes, Mom?"

"Did you meet him? Did you meet my son? Your brother?"

"Yep."

"And?"

"And ... it's a long story."

"Is he coming to visit?"

"I'm not sure."

"Oh, come on Violet. You've got to tell me something."

"There's so much to tell. I don't know where to start." I am beginning to be very sorry I phoned my parents. In my distress I did what came naturally. I sought them out. But now, I wish I hadn't. I have got to end this call. I can't hurt my mom. I can't tell her Trip has said awful things about her, that I'm trying to get him to come around, that I'm not sure he'll ever want to meet her. So, I do what I can to make her happy, while sending up a silent prayer that the good Lord works this whole thing out. "Trip looks just like you. Long curly hair. And he's got a girlfriend named Kiwi. We were supposed to have dinner tonight, but … something came up. So, maybe tomorrow."

"How long were you with him? What did you talk about? I'll bet he's smart. What are his hobbies?"

I am completely overwhelmed, which is why I revert to an immature move I'd watched Basil perform just a few days ago. I hold the phone away from my mouth and speak softly. "Mom? Dad? Are you there?"

"Violet? Can you hear us? Violet? You sound so far away, like you're inside a box."

"I can't … I can barely hear you. I'll call back when I have better service. Charge your cell and turn it on. I'll try and get a picture tomorrow and send it through text. Okay? What's that?" I cup my hand over the phone and move it back and forth, attempting to create the sound of a poor connection. "Argh. Service sucks here. It comes and goes. Sorry. Love you both," I say before ending the call.

The three homeless men make their unanimous opinion known—one shakes his head, the other runs one pointer finger over the other, shaming me, and the third actually *tsks* me. I work hard to swallow the lump of guilt in my throat. "It's difficult. I'm not proud of myself, okay?" I manage, then circle a bush that looks like Jupiter, to escape their burning glare. I plop down on a bench facing a pond full of geese and dare them to judge me.

☽

I am not ready to go back to the hotel. I need to vent, but I can't call Evie, the one person I tell everything. I think of calling Fran, but refrain for fear she'd blab everything to the entire town of Front Royal. The situation is too uncertain to share any of this with Mom and Dad (hence, the bad connection). I fumble with my phone wondering who to call. Who would listen to me? Who would understand? And then it hits me. Grayson.

I hesitate, wondering if this will be a mistake like it had been to call Mom and Dad. I haven't heard from him since I sent the smiley face. I find his name in my contacts and gently tap my finger on his name. Then I cancel the call. I do this three times before I let it connect.

"Violet?" he questions instead of saying hello.

I hesitate a second. "It's me."

"I thought I'd never hear from you again."

"Why? I sent a smiley." I place my head in my hand and contemplate how juvenile that statement must've sounded.

"No, you didn't. You sent me a middle finger."

"What? I did not."

"'Fraid so."

I check my texts, though I know there's no reason for Grayson to lie to me. Sure enough a brown middle finger is saluting me. "Geez, Grayson. I didn't mean to send that."

I hear a sigh of relief on the other end. "Thank God. I've felt terrible ever since I saw it."

I can't help but be somewhat pleased. "Really?" I ask far too ecstatically. "I mean, really?" I try again, toning it down.

Grayson laughs. "Really. Now, what's going on?"

"Does something have to be going on for me to call?"

"Considering how we left things ... yes."

My chest tightens. He's right. Why am I calling a man who's given me an ultimatum—come be with me on my turf or go on your merry way?

"I should go."

"Vi … you can talk to me."

I spill everything from the time we pulled out of the Inn lot in Secretsville until now. I leave nothing out. I tell him how upset I've been with him, how unfair it is for him to put such restrictions on a relationship that never had a chance. I tell him about New York, Evie and Basil. Trip. And, the fiasco that ensued at the restaurant after finding out that Evie and Trip clearly know each other well.

"How?" Grayson manages to sneak in when I pause for a breath.

I tell him Evie's now not so secret secret. Then I tell him about Kiwi. "So, my best friend and my other brother have been in an Internet relationship. Evie went to break it off but couldn't because she said the guy was married for a decade and his wife had her tubes tied behind his back. Evie didn't want to be yet another woman who hurt him." I swallow hard, realizing for the first time that Trip is the man who wanted children, that he's been married before. When Evie told me this I'd been under the impression that Victor was some random guy—not my brother. I feel terrible for him.

"When you think about it, Trip was cheating on Kiwi, and Evie has been lying to Basil."

"Yeah, but she's only been holding back because she fears losing Basil. She wasn't actively cheating on him."

"She should've been honest."

"It sounds like she was planning to end the Internet thing."

"Yeah, but still."

"You could help her, you know?"

"How?"

"Vouch for her."

"Huh?"

"Tell Basil that Evie loves him, that she had every intention of breaking it off with the Internet guy, aka Trip. That you know she would never do anything to hurt the man she loves. You do know she loves Basil, don't you?"

"Well yes, but ...."

"But nothing. She'd do it for you, wouldn't she?"

He had me there.

"This is all a big misunderstanding. Go back to the hotel and talk to them."

Grayson made it sound so simple. I wiped my face with my hand and looked around. Why hadn't I noticed how dark it'd gotten? I stand up and begin walking back the way I came.

"Thanks, Grayson."

"You're welcome."

"You're a good man. A really good ... friend."

"Yeah. Friend." Disappointment oozes through the connection.

"Grayson, I didn't mean to say ...." What hadn't I meant? Why did I call him friend? I'm certain my subconscious had some ulterior motive. Was I looking for reassurance? Baiting him to say something that'd let me know he wants to pursue a relationship with me? Had I been trying to open a door to a compromise?

"Grayson?" I say, but there's no response. I look at the screen on my phone. It reads, *call failed*.

134

☽

Five texts appear back to back—three from Evie; two from Basil.

Evie: *Where are you?*

Basil: *We are at hotel. Where are you?*

Evie: *Are you with Trip?*

Basil: *Trip says you aren't with him. That you left alone. We are worried.*

· Evie: *Vi?*

No idea why I'm just getting these messages. On way, I text, worrying with every step what I'll find when I get back to the hotel. From the sound of the texts, they are together. I'd expected Basil to check into his own room. Perhaps he has.

So, he's talked to Trip. I wonder how that went. I wonder if Mom will ever get a chance to meet her other son. I simply can't gauge anything from the texts they've sent.

Fortunately, the streets are well-lit and my small town spirit doesn't get too weirded out about being out in New York by herself at dusk. To be honest, the atmosphere reminds me of a late afternoon August storm. I happen to like storms. Especially the scent of them. Clean and refreshing. Like all the rain has made everything brand spankin new.

☽

The hotel suite is dark but for the dim light coming from the balcony and the glow of the city emanating below. The curtains are pulled almost completely closed, which is why I hear Basil and Evie before I see them. I find myself tiptoeing as I navigate through the unfamiliar placement of furniture. I swallow a yelp when I ram my shin into the coffee table, feel my way past first one queen bed, then the next.

I am shocked that I haven't heard any yelling or crying. *They must be keeping it low so the neighbors don't hear*, I think. The balcony door is open, causing a light breeze to lift the curtain. I flatten myself against the wall beside the opening and listen. I cannot make out what they are saying, but, to my utter amazement, no anger laces their words. I hear the grapefruit scooping sound (which tells me they are kissing), followed by a soft sweet laugh that only lovers share. I decide to peek outside and see if aliens have invaded.

Evie is sitting on Basil's lap. They are so close their noses are touching. They *look* like my best friend and brother. Their voices, though still low, *sound* like the people I was with only a short time ago. But ... they aren't angry. If anything, they seem closer than they were before we went to dinner. I can't stand it any longer. I pull back the curtain and slip onto the balcony.

They are so engrossed in one another, I have to clear my throat to get them to notice me.

"Violet. Thank God," Evie says, rising from Basil's lap to enfold me in one of her aggressive hugs. "We were so worried about you."

I purse my lips, place a hand on my hip. "Mmmhmm. It looks like it."

"Don't be facetious," she says. "We really were worried."

"If this is how you worry ... good for you."

Evie looks guilty. "We were more worried earlier. Before you texted."

This makes me smile.

"If something were wrong—"

"You would have sensed it," I finished for her. I've lost count of the number of times I've said these very words to Evie. When she's busy at work and doesn't call back, when she needs time to herself to sort through one of her kid's fiascos, any time it takes her a day or two to get in touch, I always tell her, "I knew something was wrong, but not too wrong. Or, I'd feel it if you were in danger, or I'd know if something were *really* awry." Something like that.

"I just needed to clear my head," I say, taking a seat in a wrought iron rocker next to Evie, who has forsaken Basil's lap for a space of her own. "So ..." I say on a sigh, "Shall we untangle the web?"

"Believe that's already been done," Basil says, and rises. "I do, however, believe we must debrief." He winks at me. "Anyone want a drink before we begin?" He returns from the fridge with three iced teas and a bag of sour dough pretzels. (In case you are wondering, yes, I packed some sweet tea from home in anticipation of high stress situations such as this. I'd heard no one up north knows what sweet tea is, and it is true. Yellows and pinks are not worthy of sweetening my tea.)

Evie and Basil take turns explaining the evening they shared after the cat was let out of the bag.

"I was confused, at first. I thought maybe they knew each other through work or something. But when Evie ran out I knew something wasn't right. Then, you," he points, "the way you said *no way* and your body sagged like a, like a popped balloon, that's when my stomach turned over. But I still could not figure it out."

"So he came after me, and I told him everything. We ended up at this coffee shop called Paradise Café. They are known for their chocolate dipped pie crust dunked in a cup of whipped cream."

"It's delicious. We'll have to be sure to get you one before we leave."

"Yeah. Maybe tomorrow, after we go to Victor's. I mean, Trip's," Evie says.

"Wait? What? We are going to Trip's place? You've spoken to him?"

Basil circles his glass of tea round and round, making a scraping noise on the iron table. I wince. He stills the glass. "Sorry."

I rub my temples. "Let's back up. You told Basil everything?" I say this not as subtly as I'd like.

"You don't have to protect her, Vi. It's all out in the open, which, by the way, I have to commend you for being such a good friend."

I feel my shoulders droop.

"Oh no," Basil says. "That's how you looked before. Is there something else?"

I shake my head. "No, no. Not that I know of. I'm just really sorry."

"You were stuck in the middle. We are the ones who are sorry," Evie says.

"Well, she is," Basil adds. "I didn't do anything."

Evie leans over and gives him a playful punch in the gut.

"Oof."

"So, you know that Evie was talking to a guy named Victor on the Internet. That she came along to meet him. That she fell in love with you on the way here and decided to break it off with Victor but then felt sorry for him when she met him face-to-face and decided it'd be a better idea to break up with him through text or some other form of social media? Which, by the way, I told her was way worse than doing so in person."

Basil is staring at Evie in disbelief.

"Oh no. What have I done? Evie? You said you told him everything."

She does not seem upset. In fact, she seems more joyful than I've ever seen her.

"You love me?" Basil asks Evie.

She nods, strands of blonde hair falling into her eyes. Basil reaches out and tucks them behind her ear. "I love you, too," he says.

I bury my face in my hand. "Oh brother," I mutter, refusing to bear witness to the kiss that follows.

"So, uhm, what's this about going to Trip's tomorrow? How are things?"

Basil acts as if I've appeared out of nowhere. "Vi. Oh, yeah."

"Yeah. It's me. The one who told you your girlfriend loves you, which, by the way, I thought y'all had covered already."

Evie grins as she looks into Basil's eyes. "We just hadn't said it yet."

"Glad I could be of service. So, anyway ..." I say, motioning for them to continue.

"Oh, yeah. Right. Anyway ..." Basil says, "Trip called. Said everything would be okay, that he wants us to come visit at his place tomorrow."

"That's it? No details? What about Kiwi?"

"He didn't mention her, and I didn't ask."

"Does he want Evie to come with us?"

"Yes ma'am," Basil says.

"And y'all are okay with that?"

"I mean, yeah," Evie says. "It's not like I ever slept with him or anything. Heck, we didn't even kiss. And the conversations we had online were all PG. We didn't do any of that sexting stuff people are doing now."

"It just seems weird."

"I know. But, it's really okay. I mean, if you think about it, you and Basil did more than me and Trip did, and y'all are related."

Basil and I wave our arms in surrender.

"Enough. That's enough of that," I say.

"God has a way of working everything out," Evie assures me. "Now, we just have to get you and Grayson on the same page."

I reach into the bag of pretzels, pull out three, and shuffle them one behind the other.

"You're fidgeting," Evie says.

Basil looks with curiosity from my hands to Evie.

Evie raises a hand to her mouth as if telling Basil a secret. "Something's happened with Grayson, probably."

I stop fidgeting and pop a pretzel in my mouth.

"Now she's refusing to contribute to the conversation. That means something *did* happen with Grayson."

I sigh and say, as I continue fidgeting, "Nothing happened. I talked to him. That's all. I told him what was going on and he said I should vouch for you." I point to Evie, toss a pretzel in the air and catch it in my mouth.

"Then what?" Evie asks, reaching in the bag and joining in the game. She catches two, one after the other, before I answer.

"Then I called him a friend and he got offended and ended the call."

Evie catches a third pretzel, tucks it in her cheek and says, "Are you serious?"

"I am."

Basil gets some pretzels. "I don't understand." He throws a pretzel in the air and misses. Four attempts later, I reach out and take his hand. "Clearly, this is not your forte."

I then instruct Basil on the technique of catching food from the air, distracting them from any further conversation regarding Grayson.

To ensure the topic stays off of my love life or the lack thereof, I tell them I talked to Mom. "She wants to know all about Trip," I mention while giving my neck a rest from pretzel catching. "Truth is, I don't know much about him."

"We could google him," Evie says.

I look at Basil; he looks at me. We both smile and nod at the same time.

"You know, both of you raise your eyebrows when you're all in on something," Evie says as she retrieves Basil's laptop.

He fires it up and types **Victor Wilson** and **Trip** in the search engine.

Immediately, a list of hits pops up. Basil scrolls, trying to decide which to click first.

"Just start at the top," Evie suggests.

Here's what we learn:

1. His name is Richard Victor Wilson III, hence the nickname Trip.
2. He owns the building he lives in. He bought it from his father, a real estate tycoon.
3. He has an extensive background in horticulture.
4. He grows and sells plants.
5. His business is called Pot of Life.

"Well, that would explain why his apartment is full of them," I say of the plants. "Evie did you know any of this about him?"

"He talked about going to a Farmer's Market of sorts. He said he loved gardening. I asked him how he gardened in New York. He said ... now let me think ... how did he put it? Something about having to be creative. Come to think of it, he was really vague about that."

"Evie, what did the two of you talk about?"

She blushes, obviously uncomfortable answering in front of Basil.

I let her off the hook. "Never mind."

"I'd like to know, too," Basil says, shutting down the laptop.

"Mainly dreams, you know, like living on a deserted island, or what it'd be like to start over, you know, like from a child, what we'd do differently. We'd talk about creating a planet, what it'd look like, how society would be different. Although we never could agree on a name for the planet; I wanted to call it Evie's Playground and he wanted it to be called Far Out. That's the kind of stuff we talked about."

Basil and I were both looking at her, arms folded, head tilted slightly to the right, observing Evie through squinted eyes as if this is the first time we'd ever seen her.

"What?" Evie asks, innocently. "I have an imagination, okay? Obviously, Victor ... or, I guess, Trip does too. I needed an escape. I mean, in the beginning we told each other *some* personal stuff, but after that, what else was there to say? No sense dwelling on the past. So, we talked about the books we were reading and things like being James and actually living in a giant peach."

I start laughing first; Evie and Basil join in.

"My word," I say, holding my sides.

As we quiet down, Basil poses a question. "I wonder why your ... our mother ... never googled us herself."

Evie and I both grunt.

"Ha! That's hysterical."

"Why?"

"Mom and Dad don't own a computer."

"How does your dad run his business?"

"Ledgers," I say, chuckling at how absurd that must sound. "Heck, my computer is eleven years old. The only thing I use it for is Word. And my IPhone ...." I point toward the hotel room where I've left it. "I just got it three months ago."

"Yeah, I finally wore her down, told her that silly flip phone was totally out," Evie chimes in.

"I dropped my flip one in the toilet, and it wouldn't work once it dried out," I explain. "I only use the new one for the basics. That's it."

"No Facebook?"

"Not this chick," I tell him.

"True story," Evie says. "I've tried and tried, but she's bullheaded."

"It's a time waster," I say. "Just not my thing. I don't think there's anything wrong with it though. I mean, I don't have anything against it.

"I guess I'm like Mom when it comes to technology. We simply aren't interested. I had to force her to take the phone I got for her when I got mine. She hikes a lot, likes to take pictures of birds. One day, she fell and twisted her ankle. It took her hours to get home. So, I used that experience to talk her into a phone. And, I told her she could take pictures with it. I taught her how to text, too. She and Daddy share it. Usually, it's turned off and tucked away in the junk drawer." I smile, remembering the day I gave it to her. "I had to tell a little white lie to get her to take it, though."

"What's that?" Basil asks.

"I had to tell her it doesn't have Internet. She'd freak if she knew it did. She's weird about that. Thinks we need to live simpler lives, that all this technology is clogging up the world with nonsense. And, well, I kind of agree."

"Humph," Basil says.

"What?"

"You're pretty old-fashioned, you know that?"

"So I've been told," I say, looking at Evie, who's said this to me at least a thousand times.

We grow quiet again and I find myself lost in thought. "Hmmm," I catch myself saying aloud.

"Whatcha thinkin?" Evie asks.

I get up, lean on the balcony. "Maybe Mom didn't want to be tempted. Maybe that's why she is against technology. Mom is so true to her word. When she promised she wouldn't take any more of a role than your and Trip's parents wanted, she meant it. She has always been a stickler for honesty. "Suddenly, it all makes sense. Our mother has lived her whole life treading water."

"How's that?" Basil asks.

"Think about it. She's been stuck. Never moving forward, always waiting for a kernel of information about her kids, drowning in a pool of guilt, paying for a decision that she's never felt comfortable with. No parents to help her—they were dead beets. She pretty much wrote her whole family off. They were all liars and drunks. A few were salesmen who *used* as much as they sold. Mom made it out of that mess, but then she got pregnant and had no guidance, so she ended up making a decision she's never been able to forgive herself for.

"And then she met Dad, and, he's taken care of her ever since. Not that she doesn't have her own identity. She's amazing. She has her fingers in lots of pies. She paints, you know? And she gardens. You and Trip must've gotten your talents from her. But she never got into any technology stuff, and she asked Dad to steer clear as well.

"And, he did. He'd do anything for Mom."

I peer down into the street, watch people move like ants over the landscape. Everyone seems to have somewhere important to go.

Behind me, Basil speaks up. "She is one fabulous woman."

"Yes she is," I agree.

"Violet?"

I turn around, lean against the balcony.

"I'm going to tell my parents about all of this. Sometimes I question whether or not I should, but, what you said about our mom being so honest and all, it's time to let her off the hook. She needs us to let her in."

I walk over to my brother and hug him.

"I hope Trip feels the same way," I say.

"He will. I'm sure of it."

"How do you know?"

"Just a feeling, I guess."

"I hope so. After all this time, she deserves to know all of her kids."

"I agree," Basil says.

We all gravitate back to the balcony wall and lose ourselves in the heartbeat of the city. I look out into the starless night and realize that, while the smog covers everything that twinkles and glows, the brightest twinkliest stars aren't really in the sky, anyway. They are in the hearts and spirits of those I love. I can't say I won't be happy to return to the moon and stars back home, but tonight, I don't miss it nearly as much. Not with the peace I've found in the people God has given me to love.

At 2:30 we decide to turn in. On my way to bed, my peace evaporates when I see I've missed two calls, both from Grayson. I do not check to see if he's left a voicemail, nor do I tell Evie and Basil that Grayson called back. I put him out of my mind completely.

Until this situation with Trip is settled, I tell myself. *Then I'll consider what to do about my feelings for Grayson.*

I crawl into bed, pull the covers up around me, and stare into the darkness. I cannot sleep. My plan to keep Grayson on the outskirts of my mind does not work. My thoughts keep circling back to him. I cannot help but be relieved that he called. I have no idea what we have going or if anything will come of the feelings I have for him, but he called. And I care.

Still, I wonder how we could ever make it work. He made it very clear he has no desire to leave his home. When I put myself in his position, I realize I feel the same way about my own home in Front Royal. Grayson simply got the jump on the ultimatum.

I was born and raised in my own heaven on earth. I know just about everyone in Front Royal, and those I don't know, well, my parents do. Somehow, everyone in our town is connected in some way. And I love it.

I love waking up in the morning and going straight to the mountains to hike, waving to all the people I know as I make the short trip across town to my favorite trail. I love the smell of honeysuckle in the summer, the crisp air in the fall, the clean white breath of winter, and the freshness after a good spring rain.

I love my Main Street, where I can sit with Dad at work or meet with friends for coffee or see a movie or get an ice cream or go to the jewelry store and antique shops not just to shop, but to spend time with the owners, who are my friends.

I love that there are paths all through town that parallel the creek, one of which leads to the library where I lose hours reading a good book.

I love our farmer's market and our gazebo where during the summer you can see a movie outside on the lawn every Thursday night and listen to local musicians on Fridays. I love our Festival of Leaves, the Wine Festival, and the annual Family Fun Day that Crazy Wylie, the ice cream man, and his Sundae Queen dreamed into existence.

I love that the gal who works the self-checkout at Martins gives me a hug when she sees me. I love that the produce manager knows what I'm looking for when he sees me enter the store, and I love that one of the stockers tells me I am beautiful every time he sees me. (No, it doesn't matter that he probably says this to others. In fact, it makes the compliment even sweeter.) I love the deep herbal scent I breathe in when I enter Better Thymes, our local health food store.

I love that we have a Blessing Box for those in need, book exchange boxes for those who love to read, and the churches ... they are so beautiful, ranging from quaint white country buildings to stately stone buildings, to brand new sprawling traditional brick. I prefer the look of the smaller churches; they remind me of my childhood. I especially like the old-book smell you get when you walk in. It never fades, at least not in the church I attend. And oh, the dinners the church women whip up and the Pancake Day the men's group puts on once a month … my mouth is watering just thinking of it.

The beauty and splendor, warmth and love Front Royal offers, well, it's better than any place on earth. It is *my* place. And I cannot fathom giving it up. I simply won't. Which is why, I suddenly realize exactly where Grayson is coming from. We both have roots that run too deep to extract from the earth where God intends us to be. This makes me sad, but at the same time, it brings a sort of peace. It's not that Grayson doesn't like me; he's simply where he is supposed to be. And it's not that I don't like him. He's perfect for me, but … roots, I suppose, can be a blessing and a curse. I sigh and snuggle into the covers, overcome with fatigue.

As I drift to sleep, I dream of Trip shaking Grayson's hand at a wedding. When I wake, I have no idea who got married, but in my confused early morning state, I reach up and touch my head, searching for a veil.

☽

Evie and Basil are already out on the balcony, talking quietly, when I roll out of bed. I am usually a light sleeper and up before the crack of dawn. Yesterday's events must've left me more exhausted than I thought. On my way to the bathroom, I catch a snippet of the conversation they are having. "It was the worst and best time of my life, really. I got two kids out of the deal, but I've paid dearly for choosing him over my family. They knew I was making a mistake."

"But you did it anyway," I say under my breath as Evie is saying, "But, I did it anyway."

I decide to take my time in the bathroom, go ahead and get a shower and fix my hair. Evie is telling a story she has shared only twice before. Now she's telling Basil. The irony that the people she's told are myself and my brothers, is not lost on me. I think about Evie's start as an adult and wonder how Basil will react. Each time I dwell on the details of her misfortune, I fantasize about finding Ashton and taking his eyes out with a corkscrew.

Evie's parents hated Ashton so much that he wasn't welcome in their home. Mrs. Parker told Evie there was something evil about him and neither she nor Mr. Parker approved. She forbade Evie to see him, going so far as to make an ultimatum. "It's us or him," she'd said. Evie bit her tongue and bided her time. She, very carefully, snuck around behind their back until her eighteenth birthday, then, minutes after blowing out the candles on her double chocolate birthday cake, she pulled a backpack she'd filled the day before from under her bed and slipped out her bedroom window.

She'd left a simple note on the nightstand: *I choose Ashton. Love, Evelyn*

Ashton got a job hanging drywall with some cousins in Maryland, so they moved from Oklahoma where Evie was born and raised. From that point forward, Evie had a snowball's chance in hell of bumping into her family.

At first, life with Ashton seemed blissful enough. They struggled as young couples do, but the bills were paid, their bellies were full, and Evie loved him. Soon, though, Ashton stopped coming home after work, choosing instead to carouse until late at night. Evie got angry. She'd demand answers that he refused to give. When she threatened to follow him, Ashton's truly evil character began to surface.

At first their fights consisted only of yelling and cussing, the sting of hurtful words. Ashton convinced Evie she was a useless, stupid, dumb, worthless, loser, fat pig. Not long after the verbal abuse, the shoving began, which progressed to hitting, which followed with apologies and flowers, which is why, to this very day, Evie hates fresh flowers in the house.

People always wonder why abused women do not leave. Evie says she believed what he said, that she wasn't capable of making it on her own, especially since, two short years after she'd chosen Ashton over her family, she'd given birth to his son, Joe, short for Joseph.

Once, Evie had tried to go home. She'd called her mother after a tremendous fight with Ashton that began over a debate as to which Kentucky Fried Chicken meal was the best, a bucket or a mashed potato bowl.

Evie admitted how wrong she'd been to have left like she did, told her mother, "You have a grandson. He's six months old now." She'd thought she heard her mother choke on some tears at that point. "Mother, I want to come home."

Apparently, the choking sound was a little congestion Mrs. Parker was getting over, because her next words were not laced with forgiveness. "Evelyn, you've made your bed, now you must lie in it. Running away will not solve the issue. It didn't when you took off from us. You need to learn to stand your ground."

"I thought that's what I was doing. You told me to choose. I loved him, Mother. Wouldn't you have done the same if Grandmother had given you an ultimatum?"

Mrs. Parker responded by hanging up the phone.

To this day, Evie hasn't darkened the door of a KFC, which is a shame, I think. Since her favorite was the bowl, I came up with my own version, just different enough to keep from triggering bad memories, yet delicious enough to feed the occasional craving she still gets from time to time.

The next time Evie spoke to her parents was when Ashton did something so terrible she had no choice but to swallow her own salty tears and all but drown in shame and guilt.

It was mid-July. The carnival was in town; Evie was four months pregnant with her daughter, Kate, short for Katherine, Evie's mother's name. Joe wanted to ride the carousel, but Ashton said such a ride was for sissies, that he didn't raise no girl. Two-and-a-half year old Joe persisted, "Please, Daddy. Please, Mommy. Horsey, horsey." Evie said his blue eyes looked like little fish swimming in those tear-filled eyes. When he started crying, Ashton swatted his butt, told him to cool it, but this only made Joe cry more.

"Let's get some cotton candy? How'd that be?" Evie asked. She said she'd gotten good at diffusing situations such as this one.

Ashton grudgingly gave her the money and told her he'd be at the coin toss. She dragged Joe away from the carousel and bought him a fluffy cloud of pink cotton candy on a long fat lollipop stick and got a caramel apple for herself. She'd share it with Ashton. There wasn't enough money for two.

She'd tried to get a job of her own, but Ashton absolutely refused. "No woman of mine is gonna work. It'll make me look bad. I'm a man. I take care of the finances around here," he'd yelled on a number of occasions. Only he didn't. He drank and partied away the money they could've saved. But, that night, she was happy to be out with her family. Joe was happy now that he had cotton candy, and, when she looked across the way, she saw that Ashton was enjoying himself trying to get dimes into fish bowls. She peered upward at the prizes hanging from the tent. Where would they put an over-sized stuffed monkey in their little trailer?

As they passed the carousel on their way to Ashton, Joe tugged Evie's hand and begged, "Ride horsey." It was then that Evie made a life altering decision. "Can you keep a secret?" she asked Joe, who nodded from behind the spun sugar.

She made an about-face, leading Joe away from the fishbowl game, toward the carousel, grateful Ashton had been in such a good mood earlier that evening that he'd splurged and paid for Joe to ride all night. The carnie unfastened the chain. Children ran willy-nilly, searching out their dream horse. Evie approached as the chain clinked back in place. She knew there was no time to wait for the next ride. The carnie looked at her as if recollecting. Evie believes he must've witnessed the scene Ashton had made, because he glanced around as if looking for someone, then hurriedly released the fastener and ushered her in. "You'll have to stand next to him. There aren't enough to go round."

"Thank you," she said, rushing forward, cutting off another child to get to the last remaining horse. The other kid had to ride on the bench. Evie tucked away her shame. She wanted to do this one special thing for her child. Normally, she did not cross Ashton. She did exactly what he said, but Joe had really wanted to ride the carousel and she didn't see the harm in it. Not until the ride was over, and she ran smack into Ashton as she and Joe walked through the exit gate.

Ashton's face was purple with rage. He grabbed Evie and shook her. Hard. Her head snapped back. "Who do you think you are going behind my back?" His breath smelled of cheap whiskey, his eyes were bloodshot and wide; Evie could've bet money she didn't have that Ashton had already drained the flask he kept in the glove box.

"I just ... I didn't think ... I mean, I thought ..."

He backhanded her across the face, and, raising his voice to a feminine pitch, he mocked her. "I didn't think ..." then lowered his voice to his own venomous tone. "No, you don't think. If you had a brain, you'd be dangerous."

The carnie from the carousel approached. "That's no way to treat a lady," he said.

"You stay outta this," Ashton growled, taking Evie by the arm.

Evie was crying by then, and Joe was very upset. "Mommy," he called, reaching out with both hands.

"Ashton, please," Evie said. "Joe's upset." She tried to pry his hand from around her arm, but it was too tight.

"Let her go," the carnie said.

By this time, a crowd was forming. This only seemed to fuel the fire. "She's mine and I'll do with her what I want. She disobeyed me," he said looking straight into Evie's eyes as he said it. She felt his spit hit her face as he spoke. "And she's gonna pay."

"I don't think so," the carnie said. From the corner of her eye, Evie could see he'd been joined by three other rough looking, kind-hearted men, who wanted to help. Only problem was, they were making her life far worse. She'd really get it for this.

"See what you've done? The scene you've made," he hissed, grabbing her other arm and shaking her again. "What, do you think I'm blind? That I wouldn't see you putting *my* son on that sissy ride?"

Joe was crying hysterically now, stumbling around their feet, hollering, "Mommy! Mommy!"

"Shut up!" Ashton said, releasing Evie to smack Joe on the back of the head.

Evie looked down and watched as her son went still, the shock of the pain registering on his face. He opened his mouth wide, a string of spit connecting his bottom and top lip as he wailed, tears spilling down his face.

"Ashton, stop it! Stop it now!" She said as he drew his hand back to hit the boy again. She screamed at him so loud, she scared herself.

That's when it happened. He redirected the blow meant for Joe and belted her so hard, he knocked her down.

"Mooooommmmmmeeeee," Joe screamed, holding his hands out to catch her, the cotton candy still fisted in his tiny hand.

☽

When Evie came to, she was greeted by a nurse whose eyes were like green leaves situated in bark so lined and grooved Evie thought she was in a forest looking at a tree.

She tried to sit up, but her head ached terribly, so she decided to stay put. "Where's Joe? My son," she asked, starting to panic. "Where's my son? And my baby? Is my baby okay?" She rubbed a hand over her stomach as tears welled up and spilled over. It wasn't until she reached up to wipe her face, that she realized only one side was wet. The other was completely covered.

"Your son is fine, dear. Your mother has him. We found her number on an emergency card in your wallet. We had to go through your purse, dear. And, we did an ultrasound. Your baby girl is just fine. Heartbeat's nice and strong."

Evie hadn't wanted to know the sex, but she didn't dwell. She tucked that information away to digest later. Once she knew her children were okay, another issue took up residence where that worry had been only moments ago. "My mother. She doesn't live here."

"She flew in. Your daddy, too. He's out in the waiting room. I'll go get him."

The nurse, Trudy her nametag read, turned to leave.

"Wait," Evie called. "Why are my parents here? What happened to me? What happened to Ashton? What happened?" She kept saying what happened, crying out of one eye, her head throbbing.

"Shhh," Trudy said. "I'll let your daddy tell you about all that."

"No," Evie said. "No. I want you to tell me." She couldn't bear to hear the details from her father. They'd warned her something wasn't right. She hadn't listened; she'd run off instead. Her current circumstances were not something she wanted to hash out with them.

"Honey, there's no easy way to say this."

"Say what?"

The nurse licked her lips, bit the top one, then screwed her mouth up, and looked at the ceiling. "Lord, help me," she said.

"What?" Evie said again.

"Child, you've lost your eye."

"I've what?"

"Your left one." She pointed, returned her hand to her hip. "Came in with a stick of cotton candy poking out of your socket. Looked like a posy in a bud vase." She thought a moment. "Not so pretty as that," she corrected. "The doctor did surgery. You've been out of it for a few days."

Evie said she felt the bandage, searching for the lie the nurse had to be telling. Her eye had to be there. She knew it. She was dreaming.

"Where's Ashton?" she asked, waiting for another lie to escape Trudy's lips.

"That your husband?"

"We ... aren't married."

"He's dead," Trudy said without so much as a hint of sorrow.

Evie felt the blood drain from her face.

"The way the ambulance guys tell it, by the time they arrived, he'd been beaten to a pulp. Everyone who was questioned said they had no idea what took place."

So, the whole town knew, yet no one said a thing.

☽

During Evie's stay in the hospital, her parents took care of all the loose ends, and they were loose ends—no roots existed, not a single one in the life she and Ashton had made. Mr. and Mrs. Parker packed their daughter's belongings, waited patiently for Evie to heal, reassuring her all the while that they were so very sorry and that they'd like another shot at being better parents.

Joe fell in love with his grandparents, probably because he'd never known stability of any kind, not with a father like Ashton. Evie had tried her best, but with a man like that, it had been difficult to act like some cheerful *PTO* mom. She hadn't had the energy.

When Evie was released from the hospital, her father was waiting in a U-Haul just outside the hospital doors. Evie's mother was holding Joe's hand, walking next to the wheelchair the nurse insisted was protocol.

"I can walk," Evie said, though it'd take some getting used to. Everything looked different through a single lens.

But, the nurse had insisted, and Evie wasn't in the mood to argue. She was completely bummed that her life had turned out as it had. She was running away again, back to the place she'd run from in the first place.

She hadn't gone to Ashton's funeral. One of the cousins took Joe. Evie's mother said it'd provide closure for him. Evie wondered about her own closure, but, at the time, she was nursing enough wounds. She just hadn't been able to add the funeral to the many balls she was juggling.

So, Evie went home to Oklahoma and spent the next months getting used to being a single mother, pregnant, abused, one-eyed, and widowed. She spent some time wallowing in self-pity until one day her mother came in from outside and said, "It's a beautiful day, Evelyn. Why don't you get some fresh air?"

Evie said the happiness in her mother was irksome, so, to get away from all the cheeriness, she took her mother's advice. She ended up in the back pew of a church praying to God for guidance, but when she said amen and left, she felt no different. No peace. No direction. She simply placed one foot in front of the other with no place in particular to go. She walked streets imprinted in her memory from childhood and realized that all the houses were so much smaller than they'd looked when she was little. Was it because she was looking at them with only one eye, or was it because she was an adult who'd seen too much?

Evie stopped at a convenience store located in the center of the neighborhood where she lived, and bought a water. Tired, she sat on the bench outside and listened to the hum of lawnmowers and bees. She finished her water and stood to leave just as the store clerk came out gripping a teenaged girl's arm. "You are a thief. Get out. And don't come back. Next time, I'll call the police."

The clerk disappeared inside, leaving Evie alone with a disheveled, rather intimidating girl who squared her shoulders, poked out her chin and dared Evie to engage.

"Whatchoo lookin at?"

Evie said she had no idea what came over her, but she closed the gap between herself and the girl, stared straight into her eyes searching for her soul and said, "I'm looking at a frightened child who's puttin on a big show."

"Lady, I could knock you into the middle of next week," the girl threatened.

"Oh yeah?" Evie goaded. "I'd like to see you try."

Evie told me she never knew she could be so confrontational. She'd always bowed to whatever Ashton wanted in order to avoid a problem in front of Joe. In retrospect, she learned she'd created a disastrous example for her son.

The girl reared back to wallop Evie. Just as her hand was about to connect, Evie caught the girl's wrist and twisted her hand up behind her back, a move she'd learned on the Today show just the week before when they'd covered self-defense moves that could save your life.

"I'm gonna let go of you, and you are going to sit on this bench with me and tell me just what your major malfunction is."

Three 100 Grand bars, a chocolate milk, and grape soda later, Evie and Sarah Jane Barker parted ways.

"All I did was listen, but she changed my life," Evie always says. "That's when I knew I had to get myself together and follow God's plan for my life. He used Sarah to open a door for me."

Evie never told me the details of Sarah's story, said she promised the girl she wouldn't tell a soul. All she's ever said is Sarah's life was a mess, and it was that mess that opened a door for Evie. After giving birth to Kate, Evie took a job at the local jail in Okay, Oklahoma. She worked there for a year, saved some money, healed her relationship with her parents, loved her children, let go of the past and determined it was time to strike out on her own.

Evie's last day working at the jail, Sarah Jane Barker arrived in handcuffs. Evie spoke to her, but Sarah did not respond. Evie left a 100 Grand bar for when Sarah got out. She attached a sticky note that said, *A person who opens a door for another's future deserves a better life for herself.*

☽

Evie is just finishing her story when I join them on the balcony.

"I found my current job at the detention center through some connections I'd made at the jail in Okay.

Fortunately, I had enough money saved to move and make ends meet until I got my first pay. The kids and I lived in a basement apartment for a while.

Joe hated me for taking him away from my parents. They'd been stable at the worst time in his life. His temper got worse and worse. He started biting kids in school, picking fights. He told me he hated me, that he wished I would disappear so he could go live with Nanna and Pop.

I made the mistake of telling Mom and Dad. They came to visit. The last night they were in town we went out to dinner. I knew something was up because Mom kept dabbing her napkin at the corners of her mouth, and Dad kept rattling the ice in his glass. We were waiting for the check when Mom smoothed the napkin across her lap and asked me, right in front of my son, if he could move in with them.

"I know my mother well. And she knows me. She knew if she asked me that question in Joe's presence I wouldn't be able to say no. Not with him clasping his hands under his chin, eyes squeezed shut, begging, 'please, please, please,' the s's coming out as th's because he was missing his two front teeth.

"Anyway, I kept Kate. Let Joe go with Mom and Dad, who also took in Sarah Jane when she got out of juvie. Kate and I visited when we could, but it wasn't often enough. Joe started referring to my mother as Mom and calling me Evelyn."

Evie takes a deep breath before continuing. "The bullying began in the third grade when some kid thought it'd be funny to say Kate gave her lice at a sleepover Kate didn't even attend. Didn't matter how many times she showered or how much deodorant she used, someone was always calling her dirty, swearing she smelled like garbage, or claiming to see bugs in her hair. I talked to the parents and the principals on several occasions. They always said the same thing: "Kids will be kids." But, they assured me they'd have a talk with little jerks and certainly keep an eye out for any wrongdoing. Unfortunately, the bullying didn't end. It followed her from grade to grade.

"Then, when Kate was fourteen, she got in trouble with a boy and had an abortion behind my back. All the love and counseling in the world couldn't heal her heart. She was overwhelmed with guilt.

"She came to me one evening and said she couldn't take anymore. She begged to go with Nanna and Pop, said it'd be her second chance, that she needed to get away from all the lies that'd been told and the ghosts that haunted her soul. I felt like a failure, so I let her go." Evie smiles a sad smile. "I've always felt like a terrible parent." She shrugs, tucks her hands between her knees. "I've been trying for years to make up for my mistakes."

"You are too hard on yourself," I tell her.

"Joe says I try to help everyone else's kids when what I should be doing is helping my own."

"That's a guilt trip he uses to get money from you and you know it. Your own father told you that. And Kate knows better than to go sleeping around like she does. That is not an example you set for her."

"She says I wasn't around enough, that she acted the way she did to try and get my attention. That she was trying to be like the kids I love working with."

"You were a single mother working two jobs to make ends meet. It just so happens that one of those jobs is helping other kids. Kate manipulates you just like Joe.

They are both adults now, old enough to take care of themselves, yet their main job seems to be trying to guilt you into taking care of them. You did the best you could. You sent money, you visited them, you begged to have them every summer. But nooo. If they didn't have an excuse, your mother came up with one for them.

"You are a good person, Eaves. From all that you've told me about Ashton, I think your kids act like their father."

"They didn't know him."

"Turd must be a gene, then," I say, then follow with, "I'm sorry." I look at Basil. "What Evie is not telling you is that she still tries very hard to be a part of their lives and all they do is take advantage of her. I hate it for her. Granted, their lives were rocky, but it wasn't for a lack of love and care on Evie's part. She is a great mother. Too darn giving. But a great mother. And a wonderful friend." I reach out and grab her hand.

"A great girlfriend, too," Basil says. "Thanks for sharing all that."

"You still want me?"

Basil leans in and kisses her on the cheek. "You bet I do."

☽

I keep the promise I made to myself and do not check my voicemail, although I did check to see that Grayson left two, one for each call. The three of us have a light cereal and fruit breakfast in the hotel dining room. Well, Evie and I do. Basil has three heaping bowls of Cap'n Crunch.

"It's my favorite," he says, refilling his bowl.

"Mine too," I say, "but I don't eat an entire box at one sitting."

"I'm a growing boy," he teases.

"At least put a banana on it."

"On the side," he says, pulling one from a bunch.

"Those things scratch the roof of my mouth," Evie says of Basil's cereal. She takes a seat next to him and spoons a bite of Raisin Bran and strawberries.

"It's all about technique," Basil says, swallowing. "Small bites are key as is positioning the squares toward the outside perimeter of the mouth."

"Pa-lease," I say, taking a bite of Frosted Flakes and banana. "Although I have to say, there is a sort of method to eating cereal with fruit. Take, for example, what I have here. I should be able to have a slice of banana at least every third spoonful."

"Well, yes, but it's also safe to say, that's not going to happen every time. You have to consider the banana size which isn't always going to be the same."

"But, if you know the size of the banana in advance, you modify the amount of cereal."

"Or, add a banana if they're really small."

Evie is shaking her head.

"Y'all are nuts. I thought Violet was the only one who comes up with such stuff."

"That's before you knew I had brothers." I think for a second and add, "And, yes you did know other people come up with what you think of as *weird*. You talked to Trip about creating worlds on other planets. Either the both of you were high, or y'all are just as nuts."

"Touché," Basil says, opting to forego a fourth bowl since we are planning to go to Paradise Café after we leave Trip's.

The light banter is a nice shift from the serious topic of Evie's past. Only once does she return to the subject. "You really can't tell I have a glass eye?"

"I mean ... well ..." Basil stammers.

"I don't notice it at all, anymore," I tell her. "In the beginning, I did. We've talked about it before. You notice when something or someone is different. That doesn't mean it's a bad thing. You are beautiful inside and out, Eaves."

"Well said," Basil agrees.

"Sorry I put you on the spot," Evie says.

"Do not apologize, okay?" I say. "That's part of the problem. Quit being so darn hard on yourself."

"Okay. I'm sorr—"

"No," I hold up a hand, stopping her.

"Habit," she says.

"Bad one," I say smiling. "But please don't apologize for it."

"Okay."

"Shall we?" I ask, throwing my napkin in the trashcan behind me.

Basil stands, takes Evie's hand and kisses it. "We shall."

"Here's to no more surprises," I say lifting my last sip of orange juice.

The dull sound of plastic tapping plastic is less satisfying that the clink of wine glasses, but it seals the toast. The pulp at the bottom is thick enough to chew, more of a bite than a drink. Discreetly, I turn away from the table and spit the fleshy chunks back into my glass, all the while praying this isn't a bad omen.

☽

"Come in," Trip says, stepping aside to allow room for us to enter.

"Thanks for having us," I say mechanically.

"You are quite welcome."

Basil motions for Evie to go ahead of him, his hand grazing the small of her back.

"Ya know, Trip, you have a lovely home. I didn't mention it last time," I say, scanning the jungle before me.

"Again, thank you."

An awkward silence ensues.

"Won't you take a seat?" Trip offers formally, an attitude totally unlike the energy he's exhibited in the little time I've spent with him. He seats himself in an overstuffed chair dotted with seagulls, something else I hadn't noticed last time we were here. It's difficult to notice anything but plants. Evie, Basil, and I perch on the edge of the black leather couch, grackles on a telephone wire. *Caw caw*, I think to myself as I rub my knees nervously.

"Sure is warm out for April," Evie says.

"Gonna be a hot summer," Basil mutters, taking her hand and twisting a silver birthstone ring she's worn ever since I've known her.

"So ...." I say.

"Yeah," Basil mutters.

Another long uncomfortable silence.

"Oh, for goodness' sake," Evie blurts. "This is terrible."

Trip groans. "For some reason, I thought today's meeting would be easier."

"Well, it's not. Okay? So, get over it. All of you," Evie says, taking the reins. "Last night was weird. Trip and I used to be Internet buddies. Clearly, he was keeping Kiwi from me. I, on the other hand, fell in love with Basil on the way here. I was not honest with him when we met. So, that makes us even. I'm really sorry if I messed things up with you and Kiwi.

"As for you three … you've gotta work this thing out," she says circling a finger as if our dilemma is situated in a pot at our center and she's adding the key ingredient: truth. "You are adults. And you're family. This isn't terrible. Work it out."

Silence.

Trip studies the birds on his chair.

"How is Kiwi?" I ask.

"Actually, she's fine. We didn't break up. But, she's not really talking to me right now."

Evie's phone vibrates in her pocket. She checks the number.

"Sorry guys, I've got to take this. It's work."

She steps into the hallway. "Hello," she says, closing the door behind her.

"So …." I say.

"Yeah …." Basil follows.

Trip draws in a heaving breath. "Look, I'm really weirded out by all this."

"We understand," I assure him. "Believe me, I never thought I'd be sharing my mom with two brothers."

Silence. Silence. Silence.

"Funny story. We did a little research on you."

"Yeah?"

The tension feels like a tug-of-war rope pulled tight.

Basil comes to the rescue with that easy way he has about him. "Think we can just hang out a while. Talk like friends? Maybe get a tour of this business of yours? It sounds amazing. A rooftop greenhouse," he says, appreciating our brother's talent.

And, just like that, Trip is smiling. Basil has potentially saved the day.

"You can see all the plants in here," Trip says, standing. "But the bulk of it is up there." He points to the roof. "It's why I chose the top floor apartment. That, and I feel like I don't need to cut out time for exercise what with all the stairs I walk every day." He flexes his right calf. "I don't have calves. I have cows."

Basil and I both chuckle. "I thought that was a Virginia joke," I say.

"Nope. Guess the country mouse and the city mouse share that one." He makes his way to a pull string in the hall. "I'll just leave these stairs down so Evie can find us."

We make our way up the rickety stairs to a red door. There is nowhere to stand. In fact, I have to wait my turn on the ladder, then hoist myself up and through the door on barely an inch of ledge. Basil does the same, knocking into the back of me.

Trip is far more relaxed now that he has something to do. I have to admit, making small talk around a coffee table wasn't cutting it.

"Need an upgrade on that staircase little brother," Basil says.

"Nah," Trip disagrees. "It's my burglar system."

"How's that?"

"Would you have come up those stairs without me?"

"Right," I say, nodding. "I completely understand."

"Well, here it is," he says with a sweeping motion, and that's when I take in one of the most beautiful gardens I have ever seen.

For a moment, I am absolutely speechless. It is as if I have stepped out of New York and into some lush garden somewhere in the country. "You're more of a country mouse than I realized," I say making my way through the slender maze-like paths. "Basil, can you believe this?"

"It's pretty outrageous," he says.

The space on the rooftop is the size of Trip's apartment, which isn't all that small. I'd say it's not too far off from being the size of my own house, and every inch of space that can be used up here is covered with plant life. Growing vegetables—tomato, cucumber, squash, and zucchini, dot the landscape, adding just the right amount of color. He has tiny apple and cherry trees too and a few banana plants. I'd never seen one of these before. I walk past a pineapple and stop. Trip is right behind me.

"Takes three to four years to grow one. Pretty cool, huh?"

"Very cool," I say of the pineapple that is growing out of the top of another pineapple.

"Watch the hose," he warns, pointing at the ground in front of me. I disentangle my shoe from the loop I'd stepped in unknowingly and take a moment to pause and observe my surroundings. Part of the rooftop is enclosed like a greenhouse; the half I am in is open. The hose snakes through the path where I stand and disappears inside the building.

"May I?" I point to the door.

"Certainly."

"Where's Basil?"

"Back there somewhere."

Inside, the perfume of flowers overwhelms me. "Trip, this is ... this is breathtaking."

Surrounding me is every color of the rainbow. He's created petunias in striped color combinations I've never seen: purple with streaks of yellow, white with black stripes zig-zagged like a zebra. He has poinsettias, red, white, gold, and even a deep lavender, along with geraniums, impatiens, ferns, and other plants I don't recognize.

"My experiments," he says.

"This is beautiful. Mom would be so proud."

I turn to him, see him frowning.

"Violet, I'm not sure about seeing ... her."

I don't miss that he couldn't acknowledge her as his mother or even the woman who gave birth to him.

"She'll be heartbroken," I say.

"Shouldn't she have thought about that before?"

"Who are we to judge?" I ask. "We have no idea what that time in her life was like. It must've been horrifying. Some stupid guy, a one night stand, then boom, pregnant with triplets."

"I mean no disrespect, but, shouldn't she have been better prepared?"

I feel my face flush. "Let me get this straight. You want to blame all of this on Mom? I mean, I get that you're all messed up right now, finding out about Pickle and how your own mother got tangled up in the sheets with your dad's best friend. That's pretty unprepared, if you ask me. But, I'm sure you still love her. And I love my mom, too. They are human, Trip. Human. And, if you consider the two, mom was a single, young, foolish girl taking care of herself; your mom, on the other hand, had life licked. She was married to a man who paid the bills, she had you, and she screwed it all up."

Trip's nostrils flare; his blue eyes harden. He is fuming. "Don't you dare talk about my mother like that."

"Right back atcha, my friend."

Unlike the time I misused the word friend with Grayson, I absolutely know what I am saying right now. Trip is no brother of mine if he's going to say hurtful things about my mother.

I shrug past him and make my way back through the maze, looking for the door. I run into a dead end and find Basil with Evie in his arms. She is clearly upset.

"What's wrong?"

"One of her kids got stabbed."

"One of the kids in the facility?"

Basil nods.

I find myself thanking God that Evie wasn't there. But then, if she had been, maybe it wouldn't have happened.

Evie disengages herself from Basil, sniffs, and wipes her eyes. "It didn't happen at the detention center. It was a kid we've had twice before. He has a history of violence. His parents are divorced. He hates his mom. He's told me more than once he likes to get in fights so he can feel something other than hatred for the woman who wrecked their family." She lets out a frustrated sigh. "She had an affair."

The light breeze is suddenly not cool enough. Maybe it's a connection I have with these two men who shared the same space with me all those months, or maybe it's just common sense, but I know Trip is thinking about his own mother right now.

"He went through an anger management class. Last I heard he was doing well. Working with his dad. His probation officer said he'd even started spending some time with his mom." She starts crying again. "One of the officers, Larry, said two days ago Frankie picked a fight with some kid who was carrying a butcher knife, of all things. Stabbed Frankie three times in the chest." Her breath catches. "He's just a skinny little fifteen-year-old kid who's been dealt a crappy hand." She smiles through her tears. "Just before he was getting out of juvie the second time, he'd told me he wanted a cross for his gold chain. I gave him one the day he was released. The first thing he did when the guard brought his belongings was fish out that chain and put on that cross. I told him it would protect him." She buries her face in Basil's chest. "It didn't protect him."

"In a way, it did," Trip suggests.

Evie lifts red-rimmed puffy eyes to his. "How's that?"

"Is he dead?"

She shakes her head. "He's in ICU."

"But he's still kickin. Which means, if he's as scrappy as you make him out to be, he'll live."

The look of relief that floods Evie's face makes me feel a tad less angry toward Trip.

"Listen," he says, looking from Evie to Basil to me. "The past couple of days have been a whirlwind, and I'm not handling it so well. I've got a lot swimming around in my head."

Evie looks confused.

"We had some words back there." I point in the direction of the greenhouse.

"Oh?" Basil asks.

"I'll fill you in later. You guys ready?" I ask. "Which way to the exit?"

"Don't leave," Trip says. "I want you to stay."

"So you can slam my mom? I don't think so."

"So we can get to know each other, you know, sort everything out."

"Nah. It doesn't feel right," I say, folding my arms across my chest.

"I've got something that might lighten the mood a tad," he suggests.

"What are you talking about?"

"Look behind you."

I turn around, study the plants, the ground, look up at the bright blue sky, and turn back to him. "I don't get it."

He howls with laughter. Basil and Evie join him.

"What's so funny?"

"Now I know why you avoided questions about your work," Evie says.

"What?" I say, my voice shrill as the call of a Cedar Waxwing.

"Vi is clueless," Evie says.

"You're kidding," Trip says, still cracking up.

I feel like the butt of a bad joke. My cheeks get hot; I know they're as red as a beet.

"It's weed," Basil says. "I was too busy consoling my girl to realize I'm surrounded. Gosh, that smell. It's been a long long time."

"What do you say? A peace offering. We'll relax, talk everything out."

"Uhm, I can't. My job and all," Evie says, wiping her eyes. "Although it is tempting as all get out."

"What happens in this apartment stays in this apartment. I swear," Trip says.

"No. Not me. My job's too important. But I'd be happy to sit back and have a good laugh at y'all's expense."

"You down?" Trip asks Basil.

"Meh. What the heck?"

"Vi?"

"Uhm, I don't know. I've, well … I don't know …."

"You've never smoked, have you?"

I shake my head.

"Well, then it's settled. You should always smoke with someone you trust." Trip claps his hands, rubs them together. "We're family. You should trust us."

"Oh, so we're family now?"

"Look, Violet, I've already admitted I am all over the place. My whole entire world has been turned upside down. Cut me some slack, would ya?"

I sigh.

"What do you say?" Basil asks. His eyes are shining as if he's standing in front of a row of chocolate bars and knows exactly which one holds the golden ticket.

"I don't know. I mean, I don't do things like this."

"I'll be right here," Evie says.

"Who are you? Where's my best friend? Miss Rules and Regulations?"

"My kids in JDC always tell me how relaxing it is. The one time I tried it, I freaked out. Someone gave me something bad. That was years ago. Never tried it again."

"What if that happens to me?"

"I'll kill Trip if he gives you something that's anything but weed."

"Violet, I promise you will leave here the same as you came in, only the stick up your butt won't be there," Trip says.

Before I can stop myself, I punch him in the stomach.

"Oof," he grunts, doubling over.

"Now," I say, straightening my shirt and running a hand through my hair, "about that peace offering."

☽

"Watch me," Trip says, holding the long thin white wrapper between forefinger and thumb. He lights the end, takes a long draw, and holds his breath. When he exhales, the smoke comes out thick and white, and I realize I've been holding my breath right along with him. I make a mental note that weed smells like really bad incense.

I reach out to take the joint from him, but he passes it to Evie who is seated on his left. She does not partake and immediately passes it to Basil.

"So, it's true, what the kids in juvie say. That you pass to the left."

Trip grins and nods. "Sure is."

I can feel my face screw up like a question mark.

"Meh, I've heard you always pass left to keep it simple," Trip adds. "I read somewhere once that Rastafarians pass left in times of peace and right in times of uproar. I've always just followed the rule."

Basil is nudging my arm while holding his breath.

I take the joint and nervously lick my lips.

"Nah man. You gotta wipe your lips. No one wants a soggy joint."

It takes me a moment, but then I understand. I rub the back of my hand across my mouth. "Sorry."

"Now go on and take a hit. Don't want to let it burn down. You're wasting good herb."

I put the end in my mouth and inhale. As soon as I see the paper begin to waste away, I stop. All the smoke escapes my mouth.

"Not like that. Watch me." Trip takes the joint and demonstrates, then reaches across Evie and passes to Basil who obviously knows what he's doing because Trip isn't calling him on his technique. Basil taps my elbow again, Trip releases a cloud of smoke into the air, and I am, once again, holding the joint. This time I do it correctly.

Trip explains that it is okay to puff twice before passing, but no more than that. Then he takes two puffs of his own.

I exhale. "How'd you do that?"

Trip raises his brows rather than ask what I'm talking about; he's still holding his breath.

"You took two puffs and didn't let any smoke out from the first one."

Trip laughs, the smoke escaping like a sauna door's just been opened. "Comes with practice. You'll get it."

"Wait. Is this stuff addictive?"

Basil and Trip get a real kick out of this.

"Nah, man. Don't be paranoid. Look." He points to Basil who is holding an ever shortening joint out to me.

I try, semi-successfully, I think, at the puff-puff-pass, as Trip has labeled it. After that, there is a second joint of sorts, but it looks different, like a small pipe. And after that, life becomes a disjointed dream-like journey. Like mini-vacations in the bird chair.

I feel light. Relaxed.

"Feel pretty good, huh?" Trip asks. His eyes are narrow, so I try and make mine narrow too.

"What are you doing?"

"Followin the rules. Your eyes are squinty."

"Your eyes can be any way you want them," Trip explains, leaning back in his chair.

So I widen them. To do so, I have to sit up nice and straight and stick my feet out in front of me. For some reason, Evie thinks this is funny.

"Let yourself off the hook," Trip says. "No more rules."

I mimic his pose anyway, lean back in the bird chair and try to relax, but I can't. Evie is laughing. I can't let her laugh alone. So I laugh too. I laugh and I laugh and I laugh. Trip joins in. Basil is sleeping ... I think.

"Hungry?" Trip asks, rising to his feet and going to the kitchen. He brings back potato chips and oatmeal cream pies, a box of cereal that has dried marshmallows in it, and a six-pack of orange soda.

"Healthy eating? What's that?" I say of the diet I try to adhere to most days. I reach for the box of cereal and grab an orange soda.

The marshmallows seem to fizz on my tongue. "These. Are. So. Good," I say, avoiding the cereal pieces, picking through the box for the marshmallows. "So. Good."

I eat for what feels like a very long time. As I lick my fingers, I look over and catch Trip watching me.

"What?" I ask.

"What?" he mimics.

I suddenly feel embarrassed. I shrink back into the bird chair.

"Violet, it's okay. I was teasing."

I go back to digging for marshmallows. I am thinking that the marshmallows are gold. Then I remember the prize in the bottom and begin digging more intently. Eventually, I pull out a small square. I rip into the plastic and find that I am the proud owner of a unicorn tattoo.

"Look what I got," I say, holding it out for Evie to inspect. "Let's put it on me."

I hold the collar of my shirt down while Evie applies the unicorn just under my collar bone. I look down, inspecting the finished product.

"Wow. That's awesome," I tell her. "Thanks so much."

"You're welcome, pal."

"Pal. Pal. Pal," I repeat, making a gun with my finger and thumb and shooting at the birds on the chair.

We all crack up. All except Basil who is still sleeping.

Eventually, I nap. I think. When I wake up, I feel warm and calm. Trip is cooking. Evie is helping him. Basil is still asleep. I think.

I get out of the chair, test my legs. They are working just fine. My head is as clear as drops of rain in the sunshine. I feel great.

"Basil okay?" I ask.

"Yeah. He's fine."

I walk over to him, put my face to his, feel his breath on my cheek.

"What are you doing?" Basil asks. Normally, I'd jump, but for some reason, his response doesn't startle me.

I turn my face to his. We are so close our noses touch. My eyes cross to focus in on him. "Making sure you aren't dead."

"Just enjoying the buzz," he says.

I straighten. Basil sits up.

"That's some good stuff," Basil compliments.

"I grow the very best," Trip says. "Stuffed mushroom, anyone?"

We gather around the island and eat.

"These are delicious," I say.

"Why, thank you," Trip is saying when a knock sounds at the door.

Evie answers, retrieves a box, hands off some cash, and closes the door. Proudly, she plops a box labeled manna on the island before us.

"Never tried these, huh?" Trip asks me.

I shake my head.

"Evie said she wanted you to try it, that you'd planned to stop when you leave here. I told her they deliver." He opens the box. Inside are four plastic to-go mugs, with ice packs situated underneath and between. Trip lifts one out and holds it out to me.

"Oh. My. Goodness." The presentation is spectacular. Clouds of thick whipped cream so stiff the mound above the mug holds the large chocolate covered crust securely in place. "It's too beautiful to eat," I say, wondering just how to dig into such a thing.

"Here." Trip offers me a spoon and a plate. "I put the plate under the cup. It catches the mess. When the cup's empty, you have a little treat left on the plate."

"Good idea."

I've barely taken a bite of the heavenly concoction when a large black dog comes bounding through the door. Trip is immediately excited. "Geraldo!" he exclaims, dropping to the floor to love the Clifford-sized beast he is clearly ecstatic to see. His excitement fades quickly, though, and he sternly tells Geraldo to sit and stay. The dog becomes a statue. No way would Puck listen so well. I want to ask Trip just how he has that kind of control over the animal, but when I follow Trip's gaze, I see why he is suddenly somber.

"Kiwi," I say.

Evie sits quietly studying her manna as if it is a biology experiment.

"Good afternoon, all," Kiwi says, moving toward us, her long multi-colored sun dress kissing all the right curves.

She stops in front of Trip. "Victor," she says, "I've done a lot of thinking."

He looks frightened, like a kid who's about to be sick. Even his freckles seem pale. "And?"

"And, I've decided to trust you."

Trip expels a breath. "I swear it was nothing." He looks at Evie. "I mean it was something."

He looks back at Kiwi whose eyebrow has curved in that amazingly high arch I've seen before. She places a fist on her hip and cocks her head. Then she smiles. "I believe I know what you mean," she says. It sounds as if she is letting him off the hook. She looks at Evie then Trip and says, "But I want to hear it from you two."

Evie looks up, her mouth full of pie crust and whipped cream. She reminds me of Lucy at the conveyor belt after popping so many chocolates into her mouth. Her eyes are wide. She looks from Trip to Kiwi, to me, across the room to Basil, then back to Kiwi who is rather imposing up close and personal like this.

"Heawha?" Evie asks while attempting to manage the food in her mouth. She swallows hard, deposits her spoon in the remaining dessert.

"What went on between you and Victor?"

Evie wipes her hands on the back of her shorts. Her palms sweat enough to fill a pond when she is on edge.

"Look, I didn't know about you." Immediately, she glances Trip's way. "I'm not trying to put anyone on the spot or anything. I mean, Victor didn't know about Basil either. But I only got with Basil on our way here." She realizes she's making Trip sound awful. "This isn't coming out right at all. The whole thing is completely innocent."

"I want details," Kiwi says, plucking Trip's spoon out of his forgotten manna (I am wondering how one can forget such a delight as I have been feeding my face during this entire exchange.) and helps herself to a bite.

It is an afternoon of details. Evie reassures Kiwi that the entire internet relationship was completely innocent. She even goes so far as to give her book club log-on information to both Kiwi and Basil. "We were lonely," she says. "I'll admit, on more than one occasion I imagined Victor as my knight in shining armor, but then I got to know Basil."

Trip throws his hands up. "What am I chopped liver?" he jokes.

Evie and Kiwi reply simultaneously.

"No offense," Evie says.

"Watch yourself, Mister," Kiwi says.

"Look, Evie, don't take this the wrong way, but I was never *interested*, if you know what I mean," Trip explains. "I liked talking with you, but I figured the conversations would eventually fade. I never expected you'd come to New York. When I agreed to meet, I decided I'd tell you about Kiwi, but you've been hurt so many times before.

I couldn't bring myself to tell you there was nothing romantic in the cards."

"Were you gonna text her later? Because that was her terrible plan," I say.

"Sounds like the two of you were feeling the same way," Kiwi observes.

Unable to stand the silence that follows, I say, "Not to change the subject, but, which name do you prefer?" I ask, taking the last bite of my manna, while silently coveting Evie's. She has so much left.

She sees me eyeing it and pulls it closer. "I've been talking. No, you can't have it."

"Either name is fine," Trip says. "Most people call me Trip. Dad calls me Trip unless he's mad at me, then I get Victor."

"I like the name Victor," Kiwi says. "It is strong and warrior-like."

"Agreed," I say.

"And I go by Victor online. It's my business name."

"Hmm. Okay, then. So, either one."

"Meh. Trip is okay. I'll save Victor for this sassy lady," he says, reaching out for Kiwi and pulling her in for a hug.

"And every stranger you do business with." She purses her lips then breaks into a broad grin that makes her face shine like the moon.

"Are we ... okay then?"

Kiwi smirks. "Are you going to share that manna more than just a taste or two?"

He slides it over. "You can have the whole thing," he offers.

"Dang, I know you really love me, now." She takes a bite, closes her eyes and lets out a long, "Mmm. Mmm. Mm." Then she kisses Trip right on the mouth. "Our baby loves loves loves this."

"Wait. You're pregnant?" Basil says, snapping out of the quietude he's been in since enjoying our afternoon recreation. He stretches then saunters over to join us at the island. Trip retrieves the manna he put in the fridge. "Good thing you woke up. Manna's only good for a day."

"Thanks man," Basil says, pulling an edge off the crust and popping it in his mouth.

"Victor didn't tell you?" Kiwi asks.

"Uhm. No," I say, looking at Trip.

Evie looks peeved. She asks Trip, "So, when you and I were talking, you knew you were going to be a father?"

"I thought you said it was all innocent," Kiwi counters.

The seconds-old peace peels away like an off-brand Band-Aid covering a still oozing wound.

"Wait a minute," I say, holding up a hand. "Just wait."

I lick my spoon of the last drops of whipped cream and drop it, too loudly, onto the plate from which I've been scavenging. "Basil? Are you okay with things? Do you believe Evie and Trip have zero romantic ties? I mean, you trust Evie, right? Because I do. By giving you her password, she's given y'all the keys to the kingdom, so to speak. You can logon and read everything, am I right?"

Evie nods.

"But, Evie, you have to understand—the fact that you just got upset with Trip for not telling you about Kiwi being pregnant, comes off as there being something more."

Evie nods again.

"What I think is this: Evie didn't have a romantic relationship until she and Basil got together a few days ago. Trip, you got with Kiwi, I am hoping, *after* you met Evie. Before would just make you a snake."

"Kiwi and I formed a relationship a few months after Evie came into my life, yes," Trip assures us. "But, as I've said, I enjoyed talking to Evie. And, it wasn't anything sexual. It was ... a friendship. One I still cherish."

"But, Evie, on the other hand," I continue, "had work, and me, and a few friends, but no significant other. Her feelings were more … vulnerable. Would you agree?"

Everyone nods and emmhmms.

"So, it'd make sense for her to feel a little … sensitive about feeling led on, even though she doesn't care about you in that way anymore. Not that she felt love for you." I harrumph. "I'm screwing this up."

Basil speaks up. "She liked the idea of the possibility of someone in her life. It was fun imagining she had that with Trip, until she got to know me and realized I'm so much better than a keyboard and a screen."

He leans in and kisses Evie. "I believe you, I forgive the whole thing." He turns to Trip. "Trip, I'm assuming you didn't say anything to Evie about the baby because you were thinking the two of you would never meet. Am I correct?"

"That you are."

Basil makes an exaggerated effort of turning back to Evie. I can tell he is more in tune with her after having heard her story, and I am so relieved that he seems to love her even more as a result. "Your feelings are valid. Trip is a schmuck. But you have me, so he doesn't matter. I love you more every second I spend with you. Now, how about we move on?"

Evie smiles and kisses Basil. "You're the absolute best."

Basil looks across at Trip who is ready and waiting with a balled up tea towel that he throws in Basil's face. For a split second, I am concerned, but then I see the humor in his eyes. "A schmuck, aye?"

"What are you gonna do about it, little brother?"

"How do you know you're older? Maybe I came out first."

"Maybe I did," I suggest.

"Wait. You don't know?" Trip asks me.

"Nuh-uh. Until now, I never thought to ask. This has been just as much of a whirlwind for me as it has been for you and Basil. Only, we didn't have all that other stuff about Pickle ...." I stop talking. "Wait. Does everyone, I mean, I don't want to say—"

"I'm not a total scab, guys. Kiwi knows everything you all heard through the door the other day. I'm assuming you filled Evie in on the earful you received while eavesdropping?"

I feel my face redden. "Mayyybe?"

Trip's eyes harden along with his jaw. Just when I'm about to apologize, his features soften. "Joking," he assures me, yet the stress left over from the past few minutes' conversation is still present.

"I have an idea," Basil says. "Let's just be okay. I don't think there's any right way to handle all this."

We all agree. "Sorry if I made things harder," Evie says.

"No more apologies either. We are starting fresh," Kiwi says.

There's a moment of nervous agreement and a lot of avoiding eye contact. "Okay," Trip says, "This is stupid. We are all adults here. I'm starving. I want pizza." He reaches for the cordless phone hidden in a collection of cacti. "What do you like?"

No one answers.

"Do I need to roll another fatty?"

"Goodness no. I don't think I could do that twice in one day," I say. "Not that I didn't like it. I mean ... not that I loved it." I am messing this up again. "It was nice," I finish.

For some reason, this is hysterical to everyone.

I throw my hands up as a conductor might end a song. "I like a supreme on thin crust. Now, I'm going to the bathroom. When I get back, I don't want the subject to be about … what did you call it … a fatty?"

I disappear down a hallway to the crackling sound of tension dissipating on the wings of friendship and family and bonding. I can't help thinking, a few short weeks ago I'd considered my life pretty much complete. But now, I've found I have so much more.

☽

Turns out my brothers and I have more in common than the same mother. All three of us love the same kind of pizza. Kiwi and Evie decide on a small deep dish meat lovers; my brothers and I order two thin supreme.

Since the kitchen table is covered in paperwork and plants, Trip pulls stools out of the laundry room and places them around the island just before the pizza arrives. Evie and I ask for water since all Trip has is Sprite.

"I hate soda. The fizz tickles my nose," Evie says.

"Me too," I say, simply to make conversation. Evie and I already know this about each other.

"So, Kiwi," I say between bites. "Know what y'all are having? Boy or girl?"

"We decided to keep it a surprise," she says, unaware that as soon as I mention the baby her hand moves protectively over her abdomen.

"When's my nephew making his appearance?" Basil asks.

"How do you know it's a boy?"

"Just a hunch," Basil answers, reaching for a piece of chocolate pomegranate pizza Trip ordered for dessert.

"End of October. Right around Halloween," she says.

Out of the corner of my eye, I watch as Evie taps the underside of her pizza with pinky, ring finger, middle, then pointer. I can tell by the look on her face, mouth turned down and eyebrows furrowed, that she is contemplating something. I catch her eye and tilt my head, silently asking, *what*? She gives her head a quick jerk, meaning, *not now*. I focus on choosing my own dessert pizza, zero in on it as if analyzing the chocolate chips to make sure they aren't bugs, before taking a bite. I am unaware that Trip has been paying attention to the entire exchange.

"It isn't technically mine," he says.

I slowly lift my eyes to meet his. "What's not yours?"

"I mean it is, but it isn't."

"What are you talking about, man?" Basil asks, completely clueless.

"The baby," Kiwi says, looking a little disappointed. "I thought we weren't telling people that?"

Trip stands up, takes his plate to the sink and busies himself rinsing it. "Evie figured it out," he says, opening the dishwasher that is half-full of starter plants. He closes it and dots a dishrag with detergent. "I watched you." He mimes the thing I watched Evie do with her fingers. "We want people to think the baby is mine. Because, to me, it is."

"Wait. The baby isn't yours?" Basil asks.

"If the baby is due in October, Kiwi is already four months along," I say as Evie's telepathic signals take shape in my mind. "Trip and Kiwi haven't been together that long."

Kiwi lifts her chin slightly, daring anyone to judge her.

"I love Kiwi, and I want kids. My ex, she went behind my back and had a surgery so we couldn't have any. That's why we divorced," he says to me and Basil. "I was married for ten years."

Basil is clearly surprised. I am not.

"Evie told you," Trip says, nodding his head in my direction as he towels off his plate and puts it on a shelf above the stove. "Didn't she?"

"When she knew you as Victor. Yes, she did."

"And you didn't tell me?" Basil asks.

"It didn't come up. Guess I kinda still imagine Victor as someone other than Trip," I admit.

"Me too," Evie says as if I've discovered something valuable. "It's so weird."

"Well," I say, changing the subject back to the baby before Trip can get mad at Evie for sharing the details of his divorce with me, "I think it's wonderful. This baby will grow up happy and loved, I am sure."

"I am not a ... oh ... what do you people down south call them?" Kiwi searches for a word. "A strumpet. I am not a strumpet," she says.

It strikes me as very odd that Kiwi would give two hoots what we think, and I find it both endearing and amusing that she is trying to use words we *southerners* can relate to. I cannot help it. I burst out laughing, as does Evie. Kiwi, on the other hand, bursts into tears and runs to the bathroom. This is so unlike the strong proud woman I've become accustomed to in the short time I've known her.

Evie and I try to coerce her out, but Kiwi will not budge, so we post up on the floor outside the bathroom and apologize profusely for figuring out their secret. Trip and Basil steer clear.

"I'm not upset that you know," Kiwi says from the other side of the door. "I don't want you to think poorly of me about the baby. That's what's wrong."

"No one here is judging you, Kiwi," Evie says. "Heck, we don't even know what happened. It is my experience that we mothers do the best we can with the cards we've been dealt. For years I felt like a terrible mother even though most of what happened wasn't really my fault. How I handled it was my own doing, but, you know, I did the best I could at the time. And I love my kids. Some wise woman has told me at least a hundred times not to be so hard on myself." She winks at me. "I think it's time I heed her advice." She pauses briefly. "I don't want you to spend your whole life and this baby's whole life feeling ashamed or guilty. The story behind the conception is not nearly as important as the love I'm certain you and Trip will show this child."

We hear the lock click. A few seconds later, Kiwi appears, a smile as long as a fingernail moon playing across her features.

"Thank you," she says, pulling Evie up into a hug. I stand too, work out the kinks while they have their moment.

"Truth is," Kiwi says, "we weren't going to tell people because we don't want the baby to know."

"That is your business," I say. Human nature has me automatically thinking of the poor father who will never know his child, but I have no desire to judge. After all I've learned about my own family, I quickly decide that for the rest of my days I will work very hard not to judge others. "We are here for you. Your secret is safe with us."

"He took advantage of me. He's in jail now. That's all I really want to say about it if that's okay."

The vulnerability that quivers along the curves of the words as they escape her makes my own knees weak. "Oh, Kiwi," I say, taking two short steps toward her and joining the hug she and Evie are sharing. "You poor girl," I say.

"Don't pity me. I am alive and healthy and fully blessed."

I cannot help thinking, as I hold my best friend and brother's girlfriend tight, that we girls, the three of us, will bond over the beautiful life Kiwi has so bravely chosen to bring into this world—a choice I am certain I wouldn't have made. I am in awe of her strength, beauty, and confidence, all of which drew me to her from the start. A perfect woman if you ask me. Strong enough to weather the storm and daring enough to show her scars if it proves necessary to do so.

Kiwi dries her eyes and checks her makeup in the bathroom mirror.

"You look beautiful," Evie says.

"Let's go see who's come to visit," I say of the extra baritone coming from the kitchen.

Kiwi cocks her head, listening. "Oh, that's Mr. Wilson," Kiwi says. "Trip's dad."

I'd left Mr. Wilson to fend for himself after Evie and Trip outed themselves for their online affair. I'd have to apologize for running away like I did. And for overturning a rock Mr. Wilson had wanted to keep very much in place. As a result of our presence in Trip's life, Mr. Wilson had a lot of explaining to do. Explaining he'd hoped would never see the light of day.

I sigh, suddenly exhausted. I can't help feeling like I am moving from crisis to crisis these days. What I wouldn't give for my back porch, a tomato and mayo sandwich, a glass of sweet tea, and a good book. But, I am old enough not to let my wants hurt me, so I square my shoulders, paste on a smile that closely resembles Evie's and Kiwi's, and hope for the best.

))

We join the conversation just as Mr. Wilson asks Trip if he is still going to join him for a movie. When Trip says no because he has some work to catch up on, I use this information to my advantage and say we better go. It'd been a long day.

"We're leaving tomorrow," I say. "Want to have breakfast before we take off? All of us," I clarify to include Kiwi and Mr. Wilson.

We agree on 8:30 at Paradise Café, give hugs all around and say goodbye. I am three steps down the stairs when I think about Mom. I turn and run back up, all but plowing into Basil.

"Wait," I say as Trip is closing the door. "Would you mind if ... I mean, I know you haven't decided on what to do about Mom, and I'm not trying to push or anything, but ... would you mind if we get a picture together? Would that be okay?" Remembering what Mom said about Mr. Wilson wanting to sever all ties to Trip's past, I look to Mr. Wilson as I say that last part. It'd been years, though, and we are all mature adults. Still, I want him to know I respect his feelings, too.

Surprisingly, they agree without hesitation. I realize I've forgotten my selfie stick and ask Trip for his.

"Selfie stick? Why would I have one of those? I don't have a cell phone," he says, as if offended that I'd lump him in with the rest of the world.

We have a brief conversation about how completely old school he is. "If I want to know something, I go to the library."

I keep to myself how much he is like Mom.

I hand my cell to Basil because his arms are longer than mine, we all gather in, and Trip calls Geraldo to come.

"I have never seen a dog listen so well. You told him to stay ages ago," I say, squeezing closer when Basil says so.

"Got him well-trained," Trip says.

"Say sweet tea," Evie says.

The two words ring out as one: *sweetie*. Basil takes three pictures. I immediately send them all to mom, but a lack of signal causes the message to fail.

"I'll send them when I get back to the hotel," I say. I am disappointed. The pictures would make Mom's day.

We reconfirm our breakfast plan, say our goodbyes and leave.

☽

Back at the hotel, I beg off, telling Evie and Basil I'll catch up with them a little later. "I need time to wind down," I say. This is true, but I also know when a couple wants time to themselves. Especially a new couple.

"Okay, but check in," Evie says.

I hug them both. "We've come a long way in a few short days, don't ya think?"

"Feels like we've lived a lifetime," Evie says.

Basil agrees.

"See you soon," I say.

My version of winding down is sitting on a bench in front of a small pond situated in a park not much bigger than my own back yard. Okay, maybe a little bigger than that, but small in comparison to the exotic bush park I visited yesterday. The only other people in the park are an elderly woman doing tai chi on the other side of the pond and a man feeding the geese that glide across the water's surface. I'm sitting under a big shade tree. A light breeze causes goosebumps to form along my arms and legs. I shiver, pull my knees up under my chin and sit quietly.

I want to check the messages Grayson left. Hear his voice. But I am afraid of the words. What if he doesn't want to talk to me again? He hasn't tried calling since last night. What if something's happened to him? What if the voicemails are about some emergency that popped up? What if he's in the hospital?

I force myself to take a deep breath. Why let my imagination spin out of control now? If something had been wrong, my intuition would've kicked in the minute I saw I had messages.

I pull my phone from the front pocket of my purse and wrestle with the idea of deleting the messages and Grayson's information from my phone. I have been single most of my adult life. And I've been happy. Why muddy the waters?

Because he's perfect for you, a little voice inside me says.

Yeah, so perfect he begins our relationship with an ultimatum, my mind counters.

Won't hurt to hear what he has to say, that little voice responds. *Besides, you said you'd revisit the Grayson situation once things were sorted with Trip, and now they are.*

"Awww heck," I say entering my password and pressing the voicemail button before I can change my mind.

The first message is short. *Violet, it's me. Grayson. Uhm, I'm hoping the call dropped and you didn't hang up. Call me back. Please.*

So, he didn't hang up on me for calling him friend. My heart picks up a little speed.

I press save simply because I might want to hear his voice again sometime, and move on to the second message.

I'm guessing since you didn't call back you must've ended the call. Look, Vi, I didn't mean to get upset. It's just … I want more than friendship. I've never met anyone like you. And I've never acted so quickly on my feelings before. Listen, I know I sorta made it seem like you'd have to come here to Secretsville if we are going to be together. I have work here. My life is here. I just don't see another way. Such a long pause follows, I almost hit end, but then I hear a familiar chirp in the background just before he admits, *I think about you round the clock.*

I listen to both messages again, and I get angry. Before the mature me has a chance to think of a tactful response, I find Grayson's name in my contacts and call.

He picks up on the second ring. "I thought I'd really stepped in it," he says instead of hello. "I'm so glad you called."

"You listen to me," I say, fuming. "My life is just as important as yours. I may not have a job, but I have friends and family and responsibilities. And *I* love where *I* live just as much as you love Secretsville. Maybe more. So, if you think I'm just gonna pick up and come devote myself to trying to form a relationship with someone I barely know, well … you'd have a better chance of selling your socks to the man in the moon.

"I have never felt my heart so full as the time I spent with you, but I will not give up the other wonderful parts of my life for a man.

"You ought to be ashamed of yourself, acting like your life is grander and better than mine, that you're so much more important you can't step foot out of Secretsville without it falling apart. What. An. Ego.

"After the night we met, it felt like I'd known you forever. Like we were perfect for each other. I thought you felt the same way, too. But then you went and acted like a total jerk. Guess they're right … the people who say there's no such thing as love at first sight. After meeting you, I thought whoever said that had to be wrong. But then you went and did the one thing that tipped me right back over to their jaded view of love. You made me choose.

"Guess my mind wins over my heart, after all. It's telling me to cut my losses. That's what I choose. Goodbye, Grayson," I say and end the call.

I allow myself exactly five minutes to act like I'm thirteen, then I dry my tears, delete our texts and his number, put my phone on silent in case Grayson decides to call back, cross my legs Indian style, place my hands palm up on my knees and try to meditate.

Fifteen minutes and thirty-two thousand interruptions later—flies, horns, music, gnats, the smell of hotdogs, my growling stomach—I give up on meditation, and decide to walk the streets of New York a little longer before heading back to the hotel. This walk, I tell myself, will definitely include a stop at the nearest hotdog stand.

Gosh, what an appetite I've had today. And then I remember smoking that joint. That feels like forever ago. I start to feel guilty for doing something so foolish, but that little voice inside of me speaks up again. *Let yourself off the hook.* I decide to take this piece of advice, stop at a food truck, and order a hotdog *and* a piece of pizza.

"Thanks," I say to the vendor as I collect a mustard packet. I sit on the steps of a tan brick building. A deep brown oval shaped sign with gold typewriter font letters hangs above the door: **Moon & Beam Publishing**. A wave of homesickness punches me in the gut and my appetite is gone.

I think of Mom waiting to hear all the details I've learned about her son. Wondering if he is willing to meet her, to get to know her. Wishing I'd hurry up and call.

Trip hasn't confirmed a desire to meet our mother, and I do not trust that I will be able to expertly skirt this line of dialogue, so, I squash my homesick urge to call home. I can't talk to Mom until Trip has made a decision one way or the other.

Now, I feel like a bad daughter. Mom is on pins and needles, I know. She won't call me; it's not her way. But, I'm sure that, since we last spoke, she's picked up the phone more than a dozen times to make sure it's working. And, she's probably checked all four phones in the house to be certain one is not accidentally off the hook. I feel so sorry for her. I owe her something. I've got so much to offer, but not the one gold nugget she desires. Then, I remember the pictures. I nearly overturn my paper plate as I pull my pocketbook around and reach for my phone. I steady my plate and pick up the mustard packet that fell on the step below, then I key in my password and search for the photo. I flip through the pictures, noticing the similarities between me and my brothers, Kiwi's beauty, Evie's joy, and Mr. Wilson's grizzly brows and bald dome accompanied by a nervous smile. I imagine all this news has been tough on the old guy. He's been nice enough through it all, though.

I paste the best picture into the text listing the people in the photo my parents wouldn't know. *Kiwi is Trip's girlfriend. The older man is Mr. Wilson, Trip's dad, and then, Trip is the one who looks just like you, Mom. I'm exhausted. Getting ready for bed soon. Should be home tomorrow evening. Will fill you in then.* I add a heart and a smiley face blowing a heart kiss, and hit send.

I stand, say a prayer that tomorrow I receive the news from Trip that Mom most wants to hear, then I give my food to a man with a sign that says, *God Bless You,* and make my way back to the hotel.

)

The room is dark. I glance at the clock on the nightstand that separates our beds. 9:05. Basil and Evie are curled together like S's, fast asleep. I sneak around as quietly as possible so as not to disturb them, place my pocketbook next to my bed so I'll hear my alarm in the morning, then make my way to the bathroom to change. On my way back, I stub my toe on the dresser.

"Ouch," I say a little too loudly.

"Vi? Is that you? Are you okay?"

"I'm fine. Go back to sleep, Eaves."

She yawns. "We tried to wait up."

"Sorry. I should've texted. I got all flustered after I talked to Grayson. I didn't think to check in."

"You spoke to Grayson?"

I nod, then realize she can't see me too well in the dark. "Wanna go outside?"

"Sure," Evie says.

I feel my way to the curtain, pull it back enough to shed some light, and open the sliding glass door. Evie follows.

For the next two hours we debrief the way only best friends can—in fragments. We bounce from topic to topic. I tell her about Grayson; she expresses her relief for having told Basil her life story. We fume over the way Trip talked about Mom, then giggle like teenagers when we rehash the whole weed smoking experience. We pity Trip for the overwhelming changes he's encountered in such a short time, take a few minutes to feel sorry for Basil and I as well, cry over the kid Evie got the call about, worry about her own children, then circle back to Grayson.

"I did the right thing, don't you think?" I ask Evie.

She stretches and yawns. "I think so. You wouldn't be happy in Secretsville. It may be awesome, but it isn't your home."

We stand at the same time. Evie leans in and gives me a hug. "Best you cut it off before y'all got too involved. Can you imagine the break-up? You'd have come traipsing home with a darn bird."

We laugh at my track record.

"I've got your number, missy. I think you get boyfriends for their pets," she jokes. "Want my advice? Go to the humane society. You don't need a man to have a baby these days. You don't need 'em for their pets either. If you're lonely, save yourself the heartache of a failed relationship. Adopt a pet."

"You're crazy, you know that?"

"Just a little," she says.

I open the door and we head to bed.

☽

I wake up confused, look over at the clock and throw the covers back. It is 7:30 am, but it looks like midnight. The room is dark despite the fact I'd forgotten to close the curtain last night. Outside, it is raining.

Even though we are going to be late for breakfast, I have to open the door and smell the rain, which is a bit of a disappointment. It smells nothing like the rain at home. This rain smells of people and fried food, desperation and opportunity, failure and huge successes.

I think of last night, the very one-sided conversation I had with Grayson. *No regrets,* I tell myself, straightening my spine and circling my neck to relieve the tension. *Too much good in my life to focus on anything negative.*

"Better get a move on," I say to myself as I pass through the narrow space between the door and the bed to retrieve my phone. "Well, no wonder my alarm didn't go off. Darn thing's dead."

"Evie. Basil," I say as I pull my charger and clothes out of my bag. "Wake up. We are going to be late." I place the charger in my pocketbook and make a mental note to hook it up at the restaurant. "Evie. Basil," I call again.

Evie rolls over. "Good morning," she says, her voice still thick with sleep. I reach across her to give Basil a nudge, but he isn't there.

"Hey, where's Basil?" I ask, checking the bathroom and finding it empty. *So that's why their alarm didn't go off. He probably had it set on his phone, but he and his phone are missing.*

Evie sits up. "I don't know. Maybe he went for coffee."

I search for a note but do not find one. Just as Evie is about to text him, Basil rushes in, soaking wet. "Didn't mean to take that long," he says. "I woke up really early … and, uhm … felt like taking a walk."

"In the rain?" I ask.

"Yeah. It's an artist thing. Getting a different perspective," he says, but I don't buy it.

"Sketch anything?"

"Not yet. Took some pictures though."

"Ooh, let's see," I say.

I am at his side in three steps, waiting for him to whip out his phone.

He checks the time. "We need to get a move on. We're gonna be late."

"You're right," Evie says, getting out of bed and stealing a peck from her man.

I do not miss the relief on Basil's face when I let the conversation go at that.

The next half hour is a flurry of dressing and grooming, packing, checking out, and loading our bags in the bus. God has granted us a reprieve in the rain department, though the clouds still threaten as we walk to breakfast. We arrive with two minutes to spare.

Mr. Wilson is seated at the largest table.

"Where's Trip?" Basil asks, holding Evie's chair, then mine, before taking a seat between us.

"On his way," he says, handing each of us a menu. "Oh, there he is now."

We exchange hello's and good morning's, talk over the menu, order drinks, take a few minutes more to decide on food.

"Everything looks so good."

"That manna is a blessed treat. But, it's too early for something so rich," I say, just a little sad.

"Never too early for manna," Basil says.

"I don't know about the rest of you," Mr. Wilson says, "but I am keeping it light with a yogurt parfait because tonight I'm having a friend for dinner."

Without missing a beat, Trip says, "Silence of the Lambs. 1991."

"You slipped that in nicely, Mr. Wilson," I commend. "And you ..." I nod to Trip, "well done."

"Thank ya, ma'am," he says, imitating what he calls my southern accent.

We place our order and make small talk while we wait. I am a tad fidgety. I want to talk to Trip about meeting Mom, but I don't know how to bring it up. How do I ask something so important when the topics of the morning so far have been the weather and the dog yoga class we saw in the park on the way here?

"You'd think they'd cancel in crappy weather."

"Dogs need to stretch and strengthen too," Trip says. "I'm thinking of registering Geraldo."

I start to laugh but realize he is serious.

"Could you see Puck doing yoga?" Evie asks.

Trip screws up his face at the name.

"My dog. His name's Puck. An ex-boyfriend of mine is a big hockey fan."

Thankfully, before anyone can comment, Evie speaks up. "Violet, your mom is calling my phone."

"What?" I say, as she answers, and then remember my phone is dead. My heart lodges in my throat. Mom doesn't call unless there's an emergency. We fall silent and listen to Evie's end of the conversation.

"Emmhmm. Yes. This evening. Having a little breakfast first. Emmhmm. This yummy place called Paradise Café," she says. The server approaches with our food as if mentioning the name is a summons. "Okay. I'll tell her. Bye bye, Mrs. Shine."

"Your Momma was checkin in," Evie says as I retrieve my phone and charger and find an outlet close to our table. "Said to tell you to charge your phone."

"What's it look like I'm doing," I say, frustrated with myself for not being prepared for Mom's call. "Is everything okay?"

"Oh, yeah. She just wanted to thank you for the pictures and ask when we'd be home."

The pictures. I let out a sigh of relief. "Okay. That makes sense."

"What's wrong?" Trip asks.

"Mom doesn't usually call me. She likes for me to call her when I'm not busy. I thought there was a problem."

"What made her call then?" Trip wants to know.

This is a perfect way for me to slip in my request. "Because she got the picture I sent. She saw your face. And it looks just like hers. And I know she had to be over the moon excited. I'm sure she wanted to see if you've decided to ... meet her."

"Oh," Trips responds, then dives into his breakfast.

I look to Evie who shrugs then to Basil who does the same. Mr. Wilson is busy counting the blueberries in his parfait—not that I expect help from him.

At a loss as to how I should respond, I do what everyone else is doing—I eat.

The conversation consists of, "Pass the salt," and "Got any hot sauce?" until Mr. Wilson speaks up and says, "It's okay, Son. It was wrong of me to keep secrets.

I just wanted you all to myself. You should meet her. Your mother. I've spoken with Anne. She agrees."

"She does?" Trip asks. "Because I'm curious, ya know? But you're my dad, and Anne is my mom. I love you both. I'd never want to do anything to hurt you."

"There's enough of your love to go around. This I know." He looks up from his parfait and smiles at his son who nods and looks at me.

"Then, I'll meet her," he says.

I can't help it, I throw my hands up in the air and whoop for joy. The tension breaks, the clouds part, literally, and the sun peaks through. "So, you're sure?" I ask.

Trip nods. "I'm hesitant, of course. But my biggest worry was Pops here." He claps a hand on the old man's back. Mr. Wilson wiggles his grizzly brows. "If he's okay with it, I think I should go for it."

So, he's been holding out for permission.

"Woohoo!" I shout.

"See, Violet. Everything's working out. Now, if you'll excuse me," Basil says and stands. "I'll be back."

"Robocop. 1987," Mr. Wilson announces.

"I don't think Basil meant—" Evie says.

"Doesn't matter," Kiwi says.

"I can't wait to tell Mom," I say. "I think I'll call her right now. Eaves, can I use your phone?"

Basil returns to the table as I am keying in the number. "Hang on just a sec," Basil requests as he takes his seat next to Evie, a nervous energy bouncing off of him. I drop the phone in my lap and give Basil my full attention. His knee is bobbing up and down and, if I'm not mistaken, there's a bead of sweat forming at his temple.

"Basil? Are you okay?"

"Yeah. Fine," he says, his voice shaky.

I search the faces at the table. Everyone has a concerned look.

"You okay, brother?" Trip asks.

Basil looks at him as if just realizing Trip is here. "What? Oh. Yeah. Yeah, I'm fine," he says and quickly turns to scan the restaurant. "Just wait. You'll see," he says.

While we wait, I think of Mom. I can't wait to share the news with her. Trip actually wants to meet her. Basil's weird behavior is keeping our mom from the very news she's been waiting for. Something is going on with him, for sure. But, I really want to phone Mom.

Just as I make another attempt to call, Basil says, "Wait. There," and points to two servers who've come from the kitchen, trays of manna for everyone.

"That's what you've got your knickers all twisted up for?" Trip asks.

I decide now is simply not a good time to call, that I'll phone Mom on the way home, when things are less hectic and we can really talk.

"Here, Evie," I say, returning her phone, before giving my full attention to the delight in front of me. I check my watch. 9:28. Too early for such a rich dessert, but there's too much to celebrate to turn it down. "Guess I'll consider this a vacation splurge. My stomach will likely protest later, but my taste buds are jumpin for joy," I say as the server places in front of me a mug full of creamy clouds with a wedge of chocolate covered crust, a lightning bolt, fixed in the center. My mouth is watering. "Thank you, Basil. This was a good idea," I say, scooping a spoonful of heaven onto my spoon.

When Basil does not respond, I look up and find him on the ground. Did he fall out of his chair? How did I miss it? Is he hurt? No. He's not hurt. He's saying something to Evie. Sort of whispering. I lean a little closer, look at Evie, whose fingertips are sticky with whipped cream. Had she spilled hers? Was Basil helping her clean up? Then I see Evie is holding something between her thumb and forefinger. Oh no. She's found someone's dental work in her manna. I swallow hard, imagining someone's crown sliding down my throat, and realize this thought has not caused me to lose my appetite for this exquisite dessert.

"Whatcha got there?" I ask.

Evie glances my way, confused, then back to Basil who takes the sticky shimmer from her hand, clears his throat and says, "Eaves, what I'm trying to say is … I love you, and, well … will you marry me?"

I cover my mouth. This whole time I've been thinking that Basil has had an accident or that Evie's found dentures in her manna, when really, Basil has contrived the sweetest of proposals by having the chef add a ring to Evie's manna. On her plate, written in chocolate, are two words: Cloud Nine. Basil hasn't been complaining in pain from a fall or looking for something he's lost. He's been professing his love.

"Oh, Basil," Evie begins but stops short when a familiar voice, one laced with disbelief, speaks out from behind me. "Ricky? Is that you?"

)

I turn and find my parents standing within arm's reach. Mom's eyes are wide and round, her hands tight fists at her hips. She's wearing her favorite tie-dye dress, one she's had for at least twenty years and has reserved for around the house. Daddy stands just behind her, his hand reassuring and protective, resting at the small of her back. The shadows beneath his eyes and the sand paper finish along his jaw are evidence that he has had no sleep last night and no razor this morning.

"Mom? Dad?" I ask sounding like a teenager caught at a party I didn't have permission to attend. I remind myself I have nothing to hide, that it's the sheer shock of seeing them here that has me reeling. "What are you doing here?"

My mind is racing. Has something terrible happened at home? What could have caused my parents to drive all the way to New York on the very day I am to return? What could be that important? I am drawn from thought by Mom's voice. She is speaking, but it isn't to me. I try hard to focus. Dad pulls their phone out of his pocket, hands it across the table to Mr. Wilson.

"This is how I found out," Mom says.

Mr. Wilson, pale as the whipped cream in the untouched mug before him, stares at the phone for a moment. He opens his mouth to speak, then closes it. He does this over and over, tugging at his eyebrows, making sense of something I cannot piece together. It is Kiwi who breaks the tension. "Violet, would you like to introduce us to your parents?"

Mechanically, I stand up beside Mom and Daddy. I actually reach out and touch Daddy's arm to be sure he is real. It takes me a moment to begin. My mind is traversing undiscovered ground. It is on overload. My parents are here, out of the blue. And Mom seems to be angry with Mr. Wilson. Why, after all these years of doing exactly as he'd asked by staying away, does she decide to travel to New York to confront him? This will only cause problems. Trip has just agreed to meet her. And why, for goodness' sake, did she call Mr. Wilson, Ricky? I feel unsteady.

"Violet?" Kiwi says, coming around the table to me, placing a hand on my arm. Her touch soothes like a balm. I swear she has to be an angel on earth.

"Uh ... yeah. Mom. Dad. This is Kiwi, Trip's girlfriend. And," I point to Trip, "this is Trip Wilson. My brother." I look at Mom, "Your son."

Mom stops berating Mr. Wilson long enough to turn to Trip, search her mirror image and say, "I plan on huggin the breath out of you in just minute. Right now, I must deal with your daddy." She returns her attention to Mr. Wilson.

"How dare you?" she says. "Who do you think you are? I'll tell you. You are a low-life piece of scum who—"

"Mother," I say sharply, addressing her formally as I do only in the most extenuating of circumstances. "You are going to ruin any notion of a relationship with your son before it even begins."

Mom looks at me as if I've smacked her in the face. "You don't understand," she says, speaking to me with more anger than I've ever heard come from her. She wasn't this upset when, at thirteen, I drove the tractor through the garage door.

"Mr. and Mrs. Shine," Kiwi says in that smooth water-over-gravel tone of hers that immediately draws my shoulders away from my ears, "would you like to sit down?"

The hardness in Mom's eyes soften a bit at the peaceful tone. "No," she says, the edge in her voice not as harsh.

"I'm so sorry you are hurting," Kiwi continues.

I interrupt before Mom can get started again. "I think everything has just come to a head. Mom has never acted like this before. See, Mr. Wilson ...." I pause to look at him, hoping he receives the telepathic apology I am sending. "Mr. Wilson decided to break the agreement he and Mom had when he adopted our brother. He cut her out of the little bit of connection she had. Stopped sending pictures and updates, said he wanted to move on and make a break from Trip's past. He shut her out even though he and Anne had promised to include Mom." My explanation has me recanting the silent apology. I'm starting to get worked up myself.

"That's ... not ... it," Dad says.

I search the faces at the table to see if I am the only one who feels like I'm being pranked by one of those practical joke shows I've never really found very funny. Basil has hoisted himself back onto his seat but still has the ring in one hand and Evie's finger in the other, Evie has a hand on the back of her chair as if preparing to spring to my rescue, Mr. Wilson's jaw seems to have become permanently unhinged, and Trip, well, he's eaten his dessert and is reaching for his father's.

I am cemented in place, helpless, in this midst of this mess, wondering why in the world my parents have appeared out of nowhere to make a scene that has most of the restaurant listening.

"How did you come to find out, Ricky? And not tell me you knew? Why didn't you contact me? If you'd have just stepped up, I might've kept my children together."

"Wait. What?" I say, my heart racing because it seemed to know something my mind hadn't quite picked up on yet.

Mr. Wilson finally finds his voice. "I assure you, I had no idea. Not until this very encounter. Goodness knows, I've been in love with you since the night we got locked in Kmart. The one thing I didn't have the heart to tell you then was that I was already engaged to another woman. Anne and I, we tried to make a good life together, but we couldn't have kids. Or, at least we thought we couldn't. So we adopted. I'd always thought God sent me a son who could be your twin as a way of helping me through each day without you. God knows, Hardy, you were everything I never knew I always wanted."

I feel a tad faint and grab onto the back of Basil's chair. "Fools Rush In. 1997. And it's *are* not *were*. Now, Mother," I say. "For the love of everything holy, would you please explain what's happening?"

Without taking her eyes off of Mr. Wilson, she says, "Violet. Basil. Trip ...." I suspect the long pause is to create more suspense, which is not necessary. "Meet the man who made the deposit that helped create you. I once knew him as Ricky."

"You *can't* be serious?" Evie says.

"What the ...." Basil says.

"Ho-a-ly moly," Trip says, taking a bite of his father's manna.

From the looks of it, he's already had a smoke this morning. I find myself feeling jealous.

As I stand there speechless, everyone else begins talking at once. Questions are flying back and forth like lightning bolts before a summer rain, while Daddy, in a very calm, very polite, yet authoritative baritone, is explaining to Mr. Wilson that he doesn't have a snowball's chance in hades with Mom. Mr. Wilson, however, is too absorbed in making a phone call to listen to Daddy.

"Anne," he says. "You are never going to believe this. I can have children, after all. Trip is my son. My biological son!"

Next thing I know, Mom has skirted the table and has Trip wrapped so tightly in a hug I believe his freckles have darkened from a lack of oxygen.

Amid the flurry of confusion, Basil and I make eye contact. Simultaneously, we raise our brows and shrug.

"Had no idea meeting, uh ... him was part of the plan," I say, not really knowing what name to use.

"Yeah. Me either," he says, dunking the ring into a glass of water. "Before I try and digest even a piece of this, I have to finish what I started." He turns to Evie. "Love of my life," he says, getting down on his knee once again. "Will you be my wi—"

"Yes!" she exclaims before he can finish, probably out of fear of being interrupted with some other secret revealed.

Basil slips the ring on her finger and kisses her, then reaches for his manna. He takes a bite and motions for me to sit down. "Come on, Vi. Eat your dessert. Looks like we're gonna be here a while."

Kiwi hugs me then. I'd almost forgotten she'd been standing there. She whispers something soft and soothing. The restaurant chatter prevents me from hearing every word, but I make out enough to receive the peace she means for me. "... God's grace ... didn't know was missing ... found ... family is a blessing ... joyous ... love."

Kiwi is right. I hadn't known I was missing a thing, and now I find I am overflowing with a new kind of peace and love I didn't have before this journey began.

I take my seat next to Basil, eat the manna, and soak in all that is going on around me.

☽

We leave Paradise Café in one big clump of hugs and tears and promises to get together soon. Mr. Wilson, my biological father who I imagine to still be in the same state of shock as me, and, perhaps the rest of the party, stands between Trip and Kiwi, waving. Mom and Daddy are parked in the same garage as the bus. We part between levels two and three, promising to text when we need to stop so everyone can get off the road together.

"I am so sorry I have to work tomorrow," Evie says as she follows me up the steps and plops into the passenger seat.

"That's okay," I say situating myself behind Basil who hasn't said much of anything in the five minute walk from Paradise Café. "Trip says he'll come down for the wedding, and we'll come back to New York when the baby is born."

"Mr. Wilson, says he'll come for the wedding too," Evie says.

Mr. Wilson. I conjure an image of him. *My biological father. Nice enough guy, but he'll never ever be my daddy.*

Daddy: the most level-headed, fair, sweet, handsome, perfect man I've ever known. He is so kind and attentive to Mom, and so confident. When Mr. Wilson professed his love for Mom, one that had continued burning all these years, I thought that might be the moment Daddy would finally get lathered up. But he didn't. He very kindly pulled Mom a little closer, leaned forward, and said, "I'm so very sorry you and your wife divorced. Me and mine, however, are supremely happy and content."

Mr. Wilson had apologized but then gestured toward Mom and followed with, "Still, my pulse races at the sight of this beauty."

That's when Daddy made the snowball's chance remark, so maybe he did get a little hot under the collar, but, rightfully so, I think. Not that Mr. Wilson noticed; he'd pulled out his phone and was dialing his ex at that point.

When Mom finally let go of Trip, he excused himself to the restroom. Upon his return, he was ever more relaxed. By the looks of him, it wasn't Kiwi who'd calmed him down. His eyes betrayed him; they were pink as Pepto-Bismol. He wasn't even fazed when Mr. Wilson divulged Anne's big secret.

"She was on the pill the entire time we were together. Didn't want kids at all. Said she hadn't wanted stretch marks and cravings. Anne *is* a beautiful gal," he said. "Anyway, she said she adopted Trip because I wanted a son so bad." He looked at Trip. "Said she was glad we did because she fell in love with him."

Trip smiled lazily and nodded. "Bet," he said.

Mr. Wilson continued. "She said she went away with Will to a real estate conference, one I'd sent him to for the good of our company. I thought she'd gone to the beach for the week. But she hadn't. She got sick while she was there. Strep throat. Took some antibiotic. It weakened the strength of the birth control, and, voila—Pickle."

Trip asked the server to bring a pepperoni pizza. This confirmed my suspicion.

"How'd he get the name Pickle?" Evie asks.

"Anne had him wrapped in this green blanket when she brought him home from the hospital," Trip said, licking his lips. "He looked like a pickle, so that's what I called him. It stuck. Only people who ever called him Sam were his teachers on the first day of school. He'd always come home in a tizzy, telling us how he had to tell the teacher his real name."

"Do you think it odd that Trip calls his mom by her first name?" Evie asks Basil.

I tuck away my thoughts and return to the present.

Basil puts on his blinker, follows Mom and Dad off the exit to get gas.

"Nah. Some people do that. I had a friend once who only called his dad Bobby."

"I do see the irony, though," I say.

Mom runs into the convenience store while Daddy pumps gas. She returns with coffee for everyone and asks if we're hungry.

"Heavens no," I say, thinking of the breakfast that'd turned into lunch. We'd ended up ordering more pizza; Trip ate the one he'd ordered all by himself.

Back on the interstate, we sip and talk.

"So," I say, desiring a change of subject. "When's the big day? I mean, not that you've had any time to talk about it yet, what with the family drama, which, I am so sorry about. I feel bad that all the commotion ruined what was supposed to be your special day."

Evie is quick to retort. "Oh my goodness, no. Don't think that at all. Can you imagine the story we'll have to tell? I am not upset in the least."

"A day must be picked," I say. I silently commend Mom on knowing exactly how much cream and sugar to add to my coffee, then I say, "What's wrong with right now?"

"Uhm, we don't have a preacher, and I'd kinda like our wedding to be a little fancier than me sayin I do while driving down the road in a bus," Basil says.

I punch him lightly in his shoulder. "I'm talkin about pickin a day," I say.

"Oh. Right," he says.

Upon a discussion of desires and details, we come up with the following: Evie will return to work tomorrow, as planned, and put in for another vacation, beginning at the end of her shift on Sunday.

"They won't mind," she says. "I never take time off, and they love me. And, I'll try to squeeze in all my regular massage clients. Basically, I'll work round the clock, but I can sleep on the way."

By *on the way*, Evie means a trip to Idaho to meet Basil's parents and invite them to the wedding.

I am elated that Evie is putting herself first for a change. There was a time, just a few weeks ago actually, that she wouldn't have dreamed of taking more time away from the kids who need her.

As if reading my thoughts, Evie says, "The kids will be in good hands with my coworkers. I love the kiddos I have the pleasure of working with, but ... I love Basil too. And I am so thankful to finally be completely happy. I can't wait to make it official." Then, she turns to me and says, "Vi, you'll be my maid of honor, won't you?"

Of course, I say yes. And of all the places on the road she could've asked this very important question, it just had to be right as we pass a tiny sign that reads *Secretsville*. Evie reaches back and grabs my hand.

I am overcome with a sense of love for my best friend. Her happiness is my happiness and I want to show her that. "How about you let me give y'all this wedding as a gift," I say.

Lord have mercy, the onslaught of refusal is like a war where I've been painted in a corner and sprayed with bullets in the shape of n's and o's. But I am tough and I do not go down easily. When they've emptied all the cartridges, I use the break to my advantage and speak up.

"I have the money. Evie, you never let me do anything for you. You're about to be my sister, for cryin out loud." We both squeal. "Basil, you are my brother. I want to do this. It'll make me happy. Why deny me that happiness?"

Evie purses her lips. Basil looks in the rearview mirror.

I hold up a hand. "Don't you *but* me or say anything about it being my money meant for me. You are my family. Period. I have more than enough. I know y'all aren't needy, that you'd do fine on your own. Simply put: I. Want. To. Do This. And, if you'll let me, I'll have everything worked out by the time you get back from Idaho. All you'll have to do is try on your wedding garb. I'll pick up the tab on that too. Now," I say before any more refusals can come my way. "My decision's final. The wedding and the reception are on me. And if you tell a soul, I'll quit talking to the both of you. Evie, you know how I feel about that." I cannot stand people knowing when I help others. Announcing such business is in poor taste if you ask me. Dulls the good feeling. I prefer no one knowing at all if possible. Feels better that way. But, Evie and Basil have to know.

My pause has them protesting once again.

I let them go for a minute, then, ready to play my trump card, I hold up a hand. "Do not cheat me out of a blessing."

No one ever knows how to respond to that.

That business out of the way, we start planning. We bounce from topic to topic—colors, flowers, cakes, guests, Evie's kids. We are trying to determine when to spring the news on Joe and Kate when Basil's phone rings. He glances down.

"Here, I'll get it," I say, reaching for his phone.

"No."

"You're driving," I say, removing the phone from its charger.

"I don't know that number. They've been calling for a couple of days."

"Maybe it's important," I say.

"Probably a telemarketer."

"Ooh, I have fun with them," I say, answering. Sometimes I talk with them in a British accent. Sometimes I ask them what they're having for dinner. Sometimes, I make a friend.

"Hello," I say. "Basil Montgomery's phone."

"Good afternoon. This is B.S. Waters," he says in a hoity-toity tone. I put him on speaker. "May I please converse with Mr. Montgomery?"

"Of course. Mr. Montgomery is right here," I agree, thinking this B.S. Waters sounds like anything but a telemarketer.

"It's a scam," Basil says. "End the call."

"What? How do you know?"

"End the call," he says, swerving slightly as he reaches for the phone.

"Mr. Montgomery," B.S. Waters pleads. "Thi—"

But Basil has already pressed the end call button.

"Sorry about that," he says. "I don't normally fool with a phone while I'm driving. But that irritated me."

"Why?"

"Because. Everyone who knows anything about the art world knows that B.S. Waters is the greatest curator ever. I've gotten calls like that before."

"Calls like what?" I ask.

Basil's ringtone sounds. *If you want to view paradise, simply look around and view it.* Without looking, Basil reaches down and flips a switch, silencing his phone.

"People saying they know B.S. Waters and, for a small fee, they can get my work in front of him. Crap like that."

"Yes, but this guy says he *is* B.S. Waters."

"Scammers upping their game."

I see Basil's phone light up. The same number flashes on the screen. I get this feeling in the pit of my stomach. My heart begins to race. My gut instinct is speaking up. I reach between the seats and snatch Basil's phone.

"Hello," I say, once again pressing the speaker button. Basil and I make eye contact in the rearview mirror. He is not happy.

"B.S. Waters here." He pauses. "I will assume the connection on your end was bad. Surely, no one in this day and age ends a call without saying goodbye."

"I do when it's a bogus call," Basil says.

"I'm sorry about that, Mr. Waters," I say, turning sideways to protect the phone from Basil's grasp. "It's just, well ...." I go for honesty. "Basil knows who B.S.

216

Waters is in the art world, and he believes you are impersonating him."

"No one can effectively impersonate B.S. Waters," he says. "I assure you, I am the one and only."

"Okay," I say. "My name is Violet. I am Mr. Montgomery's administrative assistant."

Evie covers her mouth to stifle a laugh. Once again, I catch Basil's reflection in the mirror. He rolls his eyes.

"Well, Violet, Mr. Montgomery's administrative assistant, are you the lovely young lady in his company the day he sketched the proposal?"

Basil glances in the mirror again, squinting this time. Evie looks back, eyebrows raised in curiosity. I shrug and continue the conversation.

"Yes. Yes this is she."

"I was the man proposing."

Basil grunts and shakes his head, clearly frustrated over what he perceives a lie. His jaw twitches in frustration. Before I can respond, he takes control of the conversation. "Bologna. That's bologna. B.S. Waters is a heavyset bald man who wears half-moon glasses and carries a pocket watch. I've seen his picture on the Internet."

"Do you believe everything you see on the Internet?" B.S. Waters questions.

"When it's on every site? Yes."

"For your information, Mr. Montgomery ... Am I speaking with Mr. Montgomery?"

"Yes," I interject, then add, "You can call him Basil." I don't know why, but I have a great feeling about this.

Basil shakes his head. He is supremely aggravated.

"For your information," B.S. Waters continues, "the fat, bald man is my assistant, Mr. Conundrum. He's sitting right here."

"Oh boy," I say. "Uhm, Mr. Conundrum? Mr. Montgomery did not mean to offend you."

"Oh pa-lease," Basil says under his breath.

"Not at all, dear. I am right portly," he says and follows with a hearty laugh.

B.S. Waters interrupts, "The sketch you gave me is fabulous, and the painting I had the good fortune of finding at the Eel Street Restaurant is breathtaking. I'm calling to set up a meeting. You, Mr. Montgomery, are the next big deal."

A quiet squeal escapes Evie as she does a dance in her seat. "This is it," she whispers. "This is the break you've been waiting for." She leans over and hugs him around the neck. Basil brakes to avoid rear-ending the bread truck in front of us.

"Sorry," Evie whispers, returning to her side of the bus while continuing to dance.

"B," Basil says, "May I call you B?" I hold the phone out so Basil's voice will be clear. He doesn't give Mr. Waters an opportunity to answer. "Sure I can. We're pals. B it is," he answers for Mr. Waters, snatching the phone while my guard is down. I listen to the fiasco that unfolds, mouth hanging open like a toolbox at a yard sale with no tools inside to fix what is broken. "Unfortunately, I've left New York. My fiancé has to work, so I cannot turn around."

"Basil," Evie hisses. "Yes you can. I'll call in. You've got to do this."

He waves at her, signaling to quiet down. "I don't have much on hand to show you, anyway. Just a few pieces. I do have some work stored at my parents' home. If you'd like to meet me, you'll have to make arrangements to see me there. This coming Tuesday. Say

11:00. 129 Doubt Street, Suspicion, Ohio. If you are who you say you are, don't call back between now and then. See you Tuesday, B." Basil ends the call and places his phone in his pants pocket, I assume, so I can't take it and pull a stunt like redialing Mr. Waters.

The hinges on my toolbox have grown rusty in seconds. I have to work to close my mouth.

"What have you done?" Evie asks.

I reach for my water bottle, down half the container and still have trouble getting my words out. I manage to echo Evie. "Basil. What have you done?"

"I had a little fun with the telemarketer," he says as if I am utterly ridiculous for asking.

"I don't get the feeling that was a telemarketer. I mean, he knew about the proposal. He has the sketch and he has the painting."

Basil's mouth turns down. I've got him thinking.

"Okay. So maybe it isn't a telemarketer. But he's a scam artist for sure."

"Why can't he be who he says he is?"

"Because. B.S. Waters wouldn't want me. I am a decent artist. I am not B.S. Water's caliber. Now, can we change the subject please?"

"Yeah. Sure."

☽

We do not speak again until Mom texts to say we are stopping for dinner. We pull off the exit and I groan. "I should've known." While the restaurant we are about to enter has delicious food, it isn't what I normally eat. I say a prayer that my stomach doesn't punish me as I seat myself between Mom and Daddy.

"I rarely get this divine opportunity," Mom tells Evie and Basil. "I cannot wait," she says excitedly.

The burgers will be greasy, the fries over seasoned with salt, garlic, and parmesan cheese. And the shakes … let's just say they will be supersized and then some.

I am contemplating a s'mores or cookies-and-cream shake when the waitress brings our menus.

The words "Oh no" pass my lips before I can pull them back.

"Hello," Evie says, poking a hand just above the table and waving weakly.

"Hey, didn't you …." Basil says, pointing in the opposite direction we've been driving.

Your Mom rolls her eyes. "Yep. Worked at the diner. Mom fired me."

"What happened?" Evie asks.

Under the table, I kick her.

"Ow!"

Mom and Daddy are looking between the three of us and up at our waitress. "You know this gal?" Daddy asks.

Your Mom talks over him. "Some idiot customer complained. Said he choked on some hair in his food. Threatened to sue."

Your Mom rolls her eyes again.

"They let you go by that name here?" I say, pointing to her tag.

Your Mom sighs, reaches up, and tugs at a piece of hair. "No choice. I legally changed it." She drops a piece of hair on the table. "Ready to order?"

Mom grabs her purse and shoves past Daddy so fast she all but tips him over. "Sea, let's go." Then she looks at us. "Well, what are you waiting for? Come on."

Outside, Basil, Evie, and I dissolve into a fit of laughter that leaves our sides aching and the previous tension over B.S. Waters a thing of the not so distant past. Basil isn't frustrated anymore, and I'm not as concerned about the whole situation. If this art curator is the real deal, it'll all work itself out.

"What's so funny?" Mom wants to know.

This leads to a retelling of the diner story.

"Her own mother let her go? Well, I don't blame her. And these idiots hired her? Must be hard up for employees," Mom says, pointing to a buffet style restaurant across the parking lot.

I breathe a sigh of relief. My insides do too. I'll be able to find something that won't leave me feeling like a ball of led took up residence in the pit of my stomach.

☽

We arrive home just as Fran is locking my door.

"How was your trip? Man alive have I've missed you. Puck and Harley have too," she says wrapping me in a hug before I can even manage a good stretch. She acts like I've been gone for months.

"And you," she says to Evie. "When was the last time you took off work?"

Fran probably knows better than Evie does when exactly the last time was she took off work. But, this line of conversation drops off when Fran sees the ring on Evie's finger.

"What's this?" Fran exclaims.

"Basil's asked me to marry him," Evie says.

A look of pure confusion crosses Fran's face. "But I thought you," she points to me, "and you," she points to

Basil who is rounding the bus to open the back and retrieve our belongings.

We smile at one another and Basil nods. Before we'd left Paradise Café, our family decided to keep no secrets from this point forward. "That didn't work out."

"Oh, I'm sorry. Oh, honey. And your best friend just swooped right in. Why, Evie, you should be ashamed of yourself."

"Well, not really," I explain, taking my bag from Basil. "Turns out, Basil's my brother. And, I have another brother too. He'll be here from New York in a few weeks for the wedding. Looks just like Mom."

Fran all but staggers backward, her hand on her heart. "Well, my word. I mean, heavenly days." She tugs her shirt away from her breasts over and over to let in air. "Oh my stars," she says, now patting her chest. "Well, I've … I've got to go. I'll be in touch."

Rumor Mill … Here. We. Come.

☽

I am sitting on the back porch sipping a cup of iced coffee, thumbing through a wedding cake magazine, and reflecting on Pastor's message regarding God's timing, when the doorbell rings. I didn't stay for Sunday school, but everyone else who would stop by my house had. "Who could it be?" I say to Puck who opens his eyes and raises his brows, then immediately drowses again. I look at the clock. 10:10.

"A guard dog you are not." I give Puck's ear a gentle tug before getting up. "Harley would scratch an intruder's eyes out before you'd even stand up," I call over my shoulder as I make my way from the porch, down the hall, and through the kitchen, place my cup on the counter on my way to the door, and make a mental note to empty the dish drainer.

As I turn the knob, I hear a chirp. My heart trips over itself.

I swing the door open to find Grayson standing before me dressed in a pair of faded blue jeans and a white polo shirt. My stomach churns when I notice he's brought along that darn canary.

He holds the birdcage out to me. "Poor guy hasn't shut up since you left."

I turn, look out at the back porch, and see Puck still lying where I left him. I search the yard for Harley and catch sight of him next door sunning himself in Mom and Daddy's driveway. I return my attention to Grayson and the bird, managing a weak smile. I simply cannot take another man's pet in place of human companionship.

"I'm sorry, Grayson, but I—"

"I'm the one who's sorry." He takes a deep breath. "Please, let me explain."

I'm so nervous I am sure he can hear my voice waver as I say, "Come on in."

"Your home is lovely."

"Thank you," I say, leading him to the back porch. Puck is not affected by the chirping bird Grayson sits in the corner.

"Please." I motion to the chair next to the wicker couch where I sit down, "have a seat."

I place a hand on my knee to keep my foot from bobbing up and down, but this does not work. My stomach feels like a beaker full of vinegar and baking soda.

"Pretty long way for you to drive."

"Violet, listen. I've been a total fool. Truth is, I'm no good at this." He motions between the two of us. "Whatever this is. I love where I live and what I do in Secretsville. My roots run too deep for me to pick up and leave, but I want to be with you."

I open my mouth to speak. Grayson holds up a hand. "Please. Just hear me out."

I close my mouth, uncertain what I would've said to begin with.

"I'm sorry I gave you that stupid ultimatum. But I didn't mean it the way it came out. I meant to show you that, well, that ... I love you. And before you say there's no such thing as love at first sight, I have to argue that my heart knows otherwise. At least, now it does. I wasn't sure that's what I was feeling at first. I mean, before, I'd have thought a person ludicrous for the notion of loving someone after getting to know her over the course of one night. But then I met you, and I've felt this incredible aching need to have you in my life forever. It wasn't until that last call, when I realized I'd likely lost you forever, that I realized the craziness in my heart that happened the moment I laid eyes on you ... that craziness is ... well, it is love."

My heart is pounding now. I am sad that my response will not be what I've imagined saying when I found Mr. Right. "As much as I want to be with you, Grayson, I can't. Not on your terms."

"Listen, I know you can't leave your home. I get that you have a life here. But I want to be with you. So, do you think it's possible for us to be together and apart? I mean live where we live but visit a lot? And not see other people because we're, well, together. If you'll have me." He pauses, looks down at his shoes then back up at me, reaches out, touches his fingertips to my cheek and says, "My happily ever after is right here in Front Royal, Virginia. *You* are my happily ever after, Violet Shine."

In three Mississippi's I am in his arms. And that's pretty much where I stay until the next morning when Evie and Basil stop over to say goodbye.

☽

"Don't worry about a thing while you are gone," I say to them, tugging at Grayson's shirt that I've thrown on over my summer pajamas.

"Good morning," Grayson says as he enters the kitchen, a broad grin on his face. "Would anyone like some coffee?"

It feels so good having him in my space searching the cabinets and drawers, familiarizing himself with my things.

Without missing a beat, Basil says, "Nah. We've gotta get on the road.

Evie, on the other hand, cannot contain herself. "Vi!" she exclaims. "You didn't tell me you had company."

"The car is out front," I say.

Evie looks over her shoulder. "Well, I'll be ... I didn't even pay attention."

"I did," Basil says, stepping into the kitchen to shake Grayson's hand. "Good to see you, man."

"You too."

Evie makes wide eyes at me.

"I'll fill you in later," I whisper. "Now," I say, speaking normally, "what has you stopping by? Shouldn't y'all have left already?"

"I wanted to see you before I left." She gives me a hug. "Wish me luck."

"For?"

"For Basil's parents to like me."

I squeeze her hard. "There is nothing to dislike."

Now I know why Evie stopped by. She needs a little confidence.

"You are gonna be just fine. They're gonna love you. I promise."

She steps back and smiles. "I needed to hear that."

"I know you did."

Evie sighs, trying on the peace she's taken from our exchange. "Change of subject," she says. "I talked with Joe and Kate yesterday. They won't be able to make it to the wedding," she says without disappointment. "But, they both gave their blessing." She goes on to say that her boss is over the moon happy for her and that she's been granted this week to travel as well as two weeks after the wedding. "I'll miss my work," she says, "but I'm just so excited and happy.

"My massage clients are a little miffed. At one point, that would have bothered me, but for some reason, I'm not at all concerned."

Basil wraps her in a sideways hug and rubs her shoulder. "Cause you're just bubblin over with love for me," he says with an accent only a local would use.

Evie gets this look of contentment about her and says, "I think you're absolutely right. Don't get me wrong, I'll worry about my kids," she says of the little miscreants in juvie, "but I've never ever felt a joy like this.

My life is perfect, and I'm gonna enjoy the stuffin out of it. I've finally found the peace I've been searching for."

Grayson brings me a cup of coffee, takes a sip of his. "Sure I can't get *y'all* a cup," he says, joining in the fun Basil started.

"Oh stop," Evie says, laughing this time. "Our twang isn't *that* pronounced."

"Wanna make a bet?" I ask. "Try listening to yourself on voicemail. I cringe when I hear my voice." It is unusual that I am making small talk with my very best friend, when what I should be telling her is that I too am happy, that Grayson and I have come to an agreement of sorts, though I'm sure she can see we've agreed on something. He's here first thing in the morning, and I am wearing his shirt for goodness' sake.

Sensing my need to talk, Evie winks and says, "Basil, I'm gonna run to the bathroom before we hit the road."

Immediately, I know Evie will find a reason for me to join her.

She's gone less than one minute before she calls, "Vi? I need some tickets."

Evie knows I keep extra rolls of toilet paper in the vanity, and I know I just put a fresh roll on yesterday. Her request is code for, *Vi, come here and fill me in.*

Just as I suspected, Evie is waiting for me in the bathroom, buttoned and zipped, perched on the vanity.

"Why didn't you call me?" she asks.

I smile and cock an eyebrow. "I haven't had time," I say.

"Oh. My. Goodness."

I sum up Grayson's visit in about half a nutshell so as not to call attention to the fact that we are gone. Not that it matters. I will tell Grayson the real reason Evie called me to the bathroom as soon as she and Basil walk out the door. But then, there won't be much to tell. Upon our return to the kitchen, Evie makes it abundantly clear that she knows what is up.

"Welcome to the family, Grayson dear," she says, stretching her words in a more exaggerated drawl than we normally use.

Grayson grins. "Thanks, sis."

Basil asks no questions, just lifts his brows at me. I glance from him to Evie as if to say, *she'll fill you in.*

"Well, we better get goin," Basil says. "I want to drop off a few paintings at this neat store out in Linden."

"You mean The Giving Tree?"

"That's the place," Basil says, following Evie out the door.

"Great place," I say. "Their produce is fabulous. So's the meat."

"They have an amazing art section."

"They certainly do. Your work will make an excellent addition."

"Oh, and we can't forget to stop and see Frankie. They're letting him out of the hospital soon," Evie says of the boy who was stabbed while we were in New York. "He's doing so well. All his wounds are healing nicely and he's getting some extra counseling." She stops on the front stoop and wraps me in a hug. "We'll talk more soon."

"Of course. Now get outta here or you won't be on the road before noon," I say, as I hug Basil.

"What's goin on with Grayson?" Basil says in my ear.

"We've come to an agreement," I say, releasing him.

"I'm happy for you," he says.

"Me too." I fold my arms across my chest. "Now, go on. You've got a long drive. And have fun," I say, watching them down the flagstone path.

"Oh, sure. Fun," Basil says, stopping mid-stride and looking back at me. "I'm going to tell my parents that I've met my biological parents and my brother and sister. And, oh, by the way, want to come to my wedding and meet them since they'll be there too?"

"Quite a mouthful," I say, waving him along. "You'll do just fine."

"You two have a safe trip," Grayson says, joining me on the stoop. I lean into him and catch that peace Evie mentioned a few short minutes ago. Grayson and I may not be a couple in the traditional sense, I think to myself, but I am certain our arrangement is perfect for us. I am content.

"Don't worry about a thing," I call to Evie. "I have everything under control. I'll text you about any decisions I need you to make."

Evie gives me a thumbs up then blows me a kiss. I catch it and send one back. Grayson and I watch as they get in the bus and take off down the road.

"I've never seen her happier," I say of Evie.

"He seems quite content, as well," Grayson says.

"I am too, ya know? Content, that is."

"Me too." Grayson slides his hands gently up my arms, rests them on my shoulders and squeezes. I tilt my head and smile up at him. He leans down and kisses me.

It is the perfect moment, really. One that is classically interrupted by my mother who hollers from her front porch, "Was Basil just there? He left a note on my door. I was in the shower. Moonbeam, who is that with you?"

She is peering, hand positioned just above her eyes to block the morning sun so she might get a better look.

"Wanna meet my mom?" I ask, searching his face.

He seems unfazed by the prospect. "I don't think I have a choice."

He's right. Mom is marching through the dewy grass in her bathrobe and slippers, a towel wrapped around her hair.

☽

The ceremony takes place in the little brick church on the outskirts of town, the one I've been attending my whole life. It is the kind of church that smells like prayers and spaghetti dinners. I love it and Evie has loved it since the first Sunday I invited her.

The organist only fudges twice on the wedding march, but no one seems to notice. They are transfixed by the bride who I just happen to be escorting down the aisle. She is dressed in a flowing ivory number all angles and edges, reminding everyone of a fairy princess. She could easily have carried a wand instead of the bunch of lavender she grips in her left hand. Her shoes are nothing more than crocheted straps that slip over her toes and tie behind her ankles. She looks like a dream. I am wearing a simple lavender dress and silver sandals. Basil and Trip wear matching gray suits and lavender ties.

The ceremony is short. The pastor sticks to the traditional vows and the "Love is Patient" Bible verse Evie and Basil requested. Fran sings "The Lord's Prayer," then disappears to the basement to oversee the food for the reception.

The weather is sunny with a light breeze, perfect for grabbing a plate of food and picnicking at the tables outside. Of course, all of the food is wonderful. No one will ever serve a better meal than one created by a ladies' church group. Chicken and ham, macaroni and green bean casserole, mashed potatoes whipped with whole milk and real butter. Makes you sing praises, that's for sure. And the desserts. Oh. My. Stars. Banana pudding. Texas sheet cake. And a strawberry Jell-O whipped cream pretzel thing. My dessert plate alone is enough food for the week.

I didn't order a wedding cake, after all. Instead, I special ordered manna for everyone. The owner of Paradise Café delivers them herself and brings along enough chocolate sauce to inscribe each plate with the words *Cloud Nine*.

The guests, friends and family both new and old, seem to enjoy themselves. Mom is the queen of all the mothers wearing her best tie-dye dress and a rainbow tiara. She's barefoot, of course. Trip's mother, Anne, and Basil's mother, Betty, share stories about the boys. Mr. Wilson stays as far away from them as possible.

Daddy is kind to Mr. Wilson. He takes him down to the pond on the church property and supplies him with one of several fishing rods he's brought along for the occasion. B Waters and his fiancé, completely out of their element, follow after Daddy. He gives B a rod, too. I stand back and watch as he tries to figure out the contraption he's clearly never used before. I make my way to the pond to help the poor guy out.

B and I have become good friends over the past two weeks. I'd called him back and let him in on Basil's skepticism, then gave him an accurate address. He knocked on the Montgomery's door bright and early, just as the biscuits were coming out of the oven and the gravy was being poured. Turns out, he is the real deal. And he's going to make Basil a gazillionaire, I am sure.

Funny story: When B called back to thank me for seeking him out before he tried to get tickets to some fake place Basil had contrived, I asked him what B.S. stands for.

"It has nothing to do with being full of *it*. Sakes alive, but I was teased in school." He paused, obviously reflecting on the painful experience. "My parents decided to take advantage of our last name. They wanted me to be a living message to the rest of the world. Beside Still is my given name."

It took a moment for me to get the picture. When I did, I was sure to stifle the bubble of laughter that so wanted to escape. Upon swallowing that laugh, I choked on the notion that B's name totally works for him. He'd certainly come through in a heavenly way for my little brother, Basil.

"Beside Still Waters, huh?"

"Yes ma'am,"

"Absolutely beautiful."

We've been texting buddies ever since.

☽

B casts the line perfectly. I applaud.

"What's made you so happy, Violet Shine?"

I do not have to turn around to put a name to the voice.

"You," I say as Grayson places a kiss on my temple. "And my family."

The wedding party and guests have made their way to the pond. Mom, Anne, and Betty are chatting under a nearby scarlet curl willow. Trip and Evie join us.

"What's going on over there?" Evie asks Trip.

Not too far away, Will and Pickle are having what looks like a heated discussion.

"Pickle loves debating," Trip says.

Pickle and his dad are all furrowed eyebrows and stern body language. Their fingers move quickly, yet firmly. Until they'd arrived, we had no idea Pickle is deaf.

"It's not a big thing to us," Trip says when Evie asks him why he'd never mentioned it. "No reason to define him by his inability to hear."

"Right. Sorry," Evie says, feeling guilty.

"No big deal."

I am beginning to understand that not much is a big deal to Trip. Unless you count the bombshell Basil and I dropped on him in New York, though it hasn't taken him long to get used to it.

"Look at the size of my family now," he says motioning to our relatives clumped like cattails around the pond. "Mary Jane's going to have so many people who love her."

Kiwi has made her way to us and has overheard. She says in her soft soothing tone, "Victor, while I heartily agree that our child is very fortunate to have so many people to cherish and love her, do not believe for an instant that she is going to be named after your favorite plant."

I laugh and turn away, taking Grayson's hand. We walk the perimeter of the pond stopping to chat or to listen as our family knits a solid foundation. Betty shares a memory with Mom and Anne. "When Basil was in the fourth grade, he and his little friend Shorty got into some mischief. Their teacher, Miss Shiffle, called to say that all the red pencils went missing from the children's pencil bags. No one could make corrections to their daily warm-ups. Come to find out, over the course of one week, Basil and Shorty stole every single one of the red pencils and hoarded them in their own pencil bags."

"We could've gotten away with it," Basil calls, overhearing his mother. "Excuse me, Fran," he says, breaking off his conversation with her to join *the mothers* as we've started calling them. "But, we'd forgotten one very important step."

"How'd you get found out?" Mom asks, completely taken in by the story.

"Shorty and I were the only ones who still had red pencils."

Everyone roars with laughter, including Grayson and I.

"I got suspended. Shorty only got after school. The principal said 'the ringleader pays dearly'" Basil mimics in a high pitched nasally tone. "And boy did I. Dad had me helping every neighboring farm for free for the next three months, didn't you Dad?" Basil calls over his shoulder to a fit looking gentleman in a fashionable suit Basil said his father had been wearing to special occasions for the past thirty years.

Mr. Montgomery skips the final rock in his hand and joins the group.

Grayson and I continue our stroll. Fran directs the ladies to begin clearing tables. Evie joins Basil. B shouts with joy when he catches a fish and then asks Daddy how the heck to get the thing off the line.

"I have to leave early tomorrow. Meeting," Grayson says softly.

I nod. We've barely been apart since he and the bird arrived. I will miss him, but I am okay with our arrangement.

"I have some commitments here for the next couple weeks," I say. "Puck has a vet appointment. The church will have to be cleaned. I promised cookies and brownies to the library for story time this Friday. And, Mom and I are going to New York to meet up with Anne so we can take Kiwi shopping for baby stuff. I think she's moving in with Trip. God help her. She'll have the baby, only to lose him in all those plants."

Grayson laughs.

We make our way past the tables where Trip and Kiwi have found a seat under a shade tree.

"Hempingway?" Trip asks.

"You are out of your mind," Kiwi says.

"What about Tokin? Tokin's a good name."

"No way."

"Blaze?"

"Nuh-uh." Kiwi is laughing now, enjoying the game she will most certainly win.

"Heidi. Get it. *High*-dee?" Trip asks, breaking the syllables to achieve the affect he's going for. "But we'll cover it up by spelling it like normal people. We can *hi*de the true meaning so that we might walk among the average unnoticed," he jokes.

"I do like the name Heidi," Kiwi says. "But what if it's not a girl?"

Their voices grow distant as we round the church.

"Ooh, we could name a boy Dabnus."

"Forget it."

"How bout Bud?"

Kiwi's laugh coasts along on the breeze like chimes and birdsong and trickling streams all wrapped up in a warm spring day topped with a multi-colored bow only God can produce with raindrops and sunshine.

I can only imagine that, when the baby is born, Trip's extra-curricular activity will become far less important. Love will do that to a person.

"When do you think you'll be able to get to Secretsville?" Grayson asks, interrupting my thoughts. I do not miss the apprehension in his voice. "I'm not trying to push or anything. I can come back here in a couple weeks if you want." He pauses in front of the church, turns to face me. "Look, I don't want to say or do anything wrong. I don't want to lose you."

I give him a kiss, touch my nose to his. "No chance of that. I love you."

"I love you, too."

"How about I come to you after Mom and I get back from New York. Say, beginning of June. I'll stay for a week or so, if that's okay."

Grayson takes my hand, leads me up the steps of the church where we sit looking out at the mountains surrounding us. I rest my head on his shoulder, feel his hand at my waist.

"That sounds just fine," he says.

We hear Mr. Wilson yell, "I caught an uncatchable fish!"

A split second later, Trip and Anne yell together, "Big Fish. 2003."

"I've decided to give him a chance," I say of Mr. Wilson. "Get to know him. Love him. He'll be like an uncle, ya know?"

"Mmmm," Grayson says, kissing the top of my head.

I run my hand over his knee, and breathe in. *So, this is what it feels like to have it all. Pleasure and peace and love: Family.*

☽

"Oh, and, Grayson?"

"Yes?"

"You're takin the bird with you."

"You aren't even going to ask his name are you?"

"Not a chance."

ABOUT THE AUTHOR

Missi Magalis is the author of *Ain't No Better Treasure; Merry Christmas, Mom and Dad; Good Morning, Mrs. Clark; Beautifully Broken; How Do You Do, Mrs. Wiley?* and *Ashmikisle Out of the Ashes.* She was born and raised in Front Royal, Virginia, and earned degrees from Lord Fairfax Community College and Shenandoah University. She resides in her hometown with her husband and three daughters. Visit her website at www.missimagalis.com.